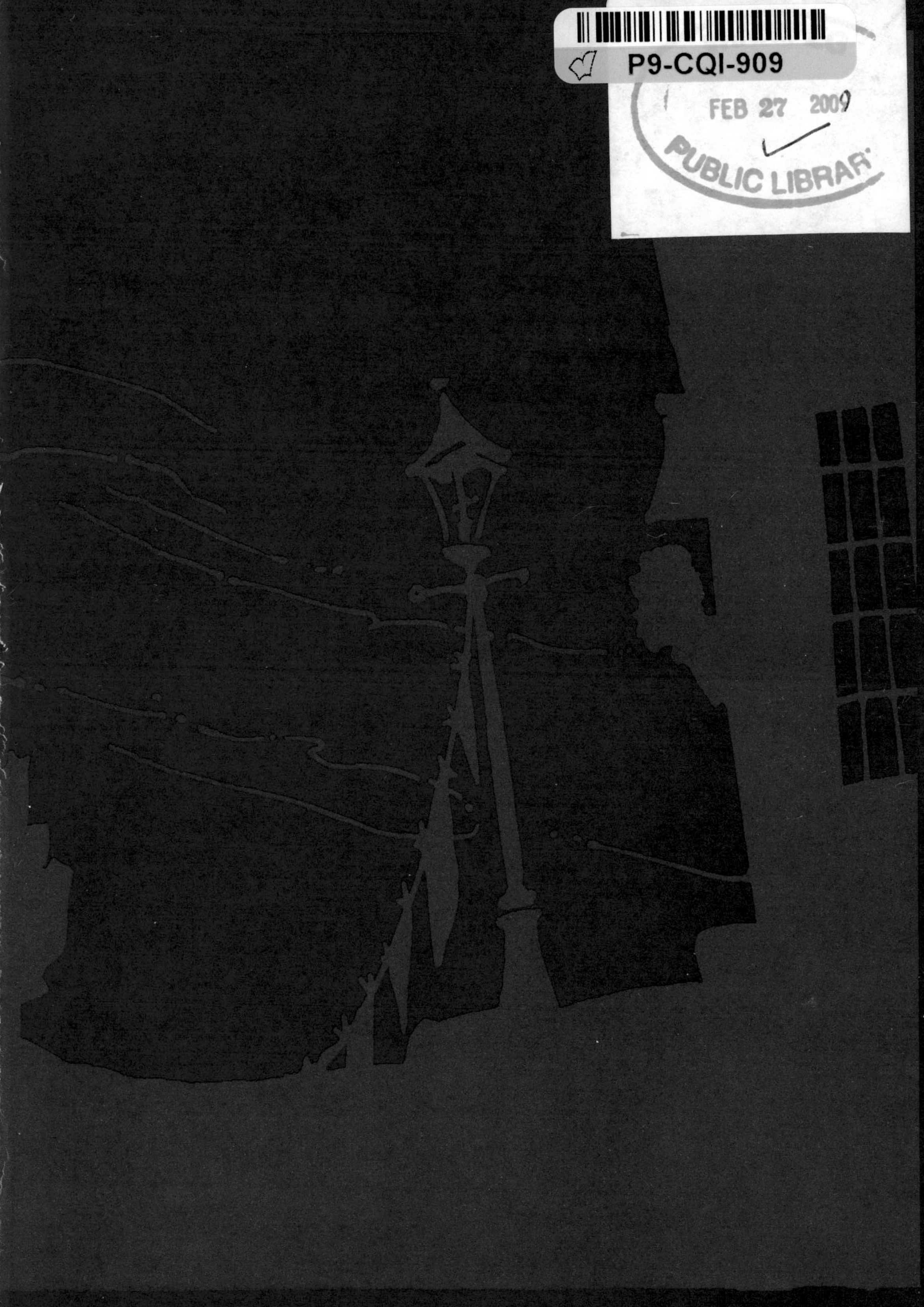

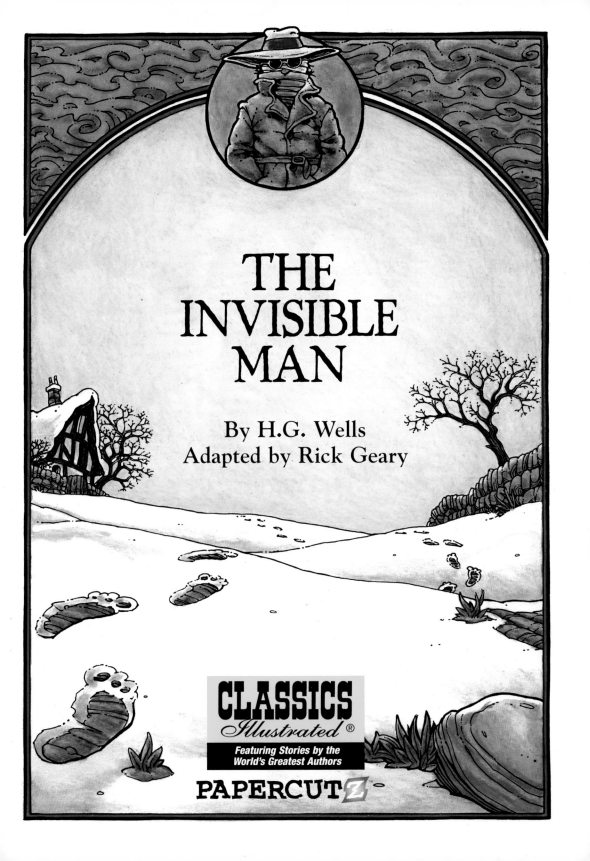

THE INVISIBLE MAN

By H.G. Wells
Adapted by Rick Geary

CLASSICS
Illustrated ®

Featuring Stories by the
World's Greatest Authors

PAPERCUTZ

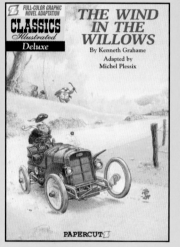

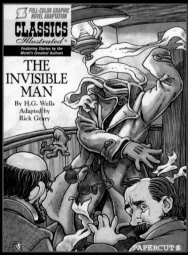

CLASSICS Illustrated ®

Featuring Stories by the World's Greatest Authors

#2

THE INVISIBLE MAN

By H.G. Wells
Adapted by Rick Geary

PAPERCUTZ™

New York

The Invisible Man
By H. G. Wells
Adapted by Rick Geary
Wade Roberts, Original Editorial Director
Kurt Goldzung, Original Creative Director
Mike McCormack, Original Art Director
Valarie Jones, Original Editor
Jim Salicrup
Editor-in-Chief

ISBN 13: 978-1-59707-106-2
ISBN 10: 1-59707-106-4

Printed in China.
Distributed by Macmillan.
10 9 8 7 6 5 4 3 2 1

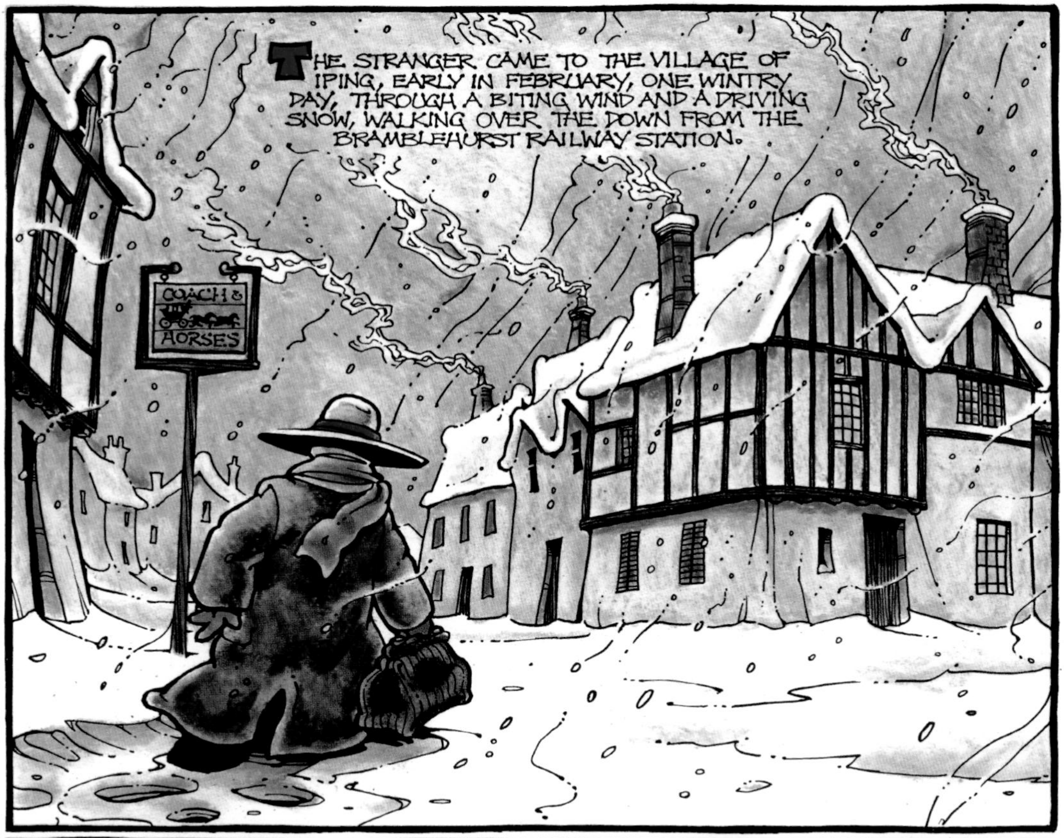
THE STRANGER CAME TO THE VILLAGE OF IPING, EARLY IN FEBRUARY, ONE WINTRY DAY, THROUGH A BITING WIND AND A DRIVING SNOW, WALKING OVER THE DOWN FROM THE BRAMBLEHURST RAILWAY STATION.
COACH & HORSES

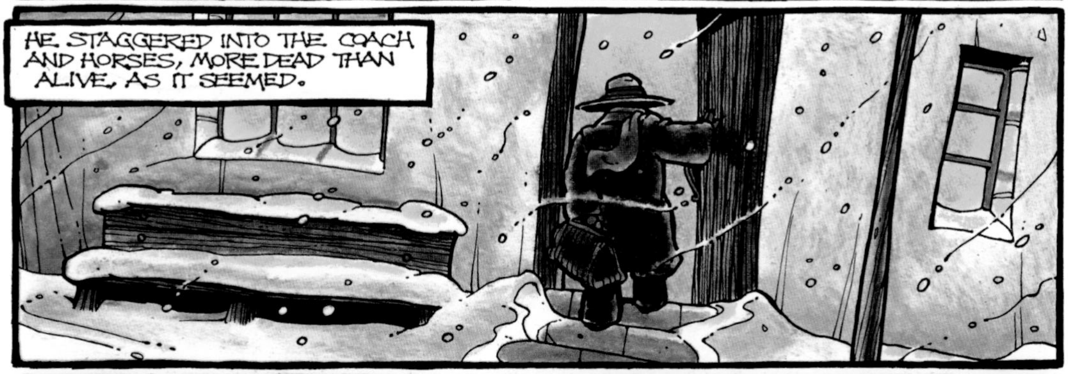
HE STAGGERED INTO THE COACH AND HORSES, MORE DEAD THAN ALIVE, AS IT SEEMED.

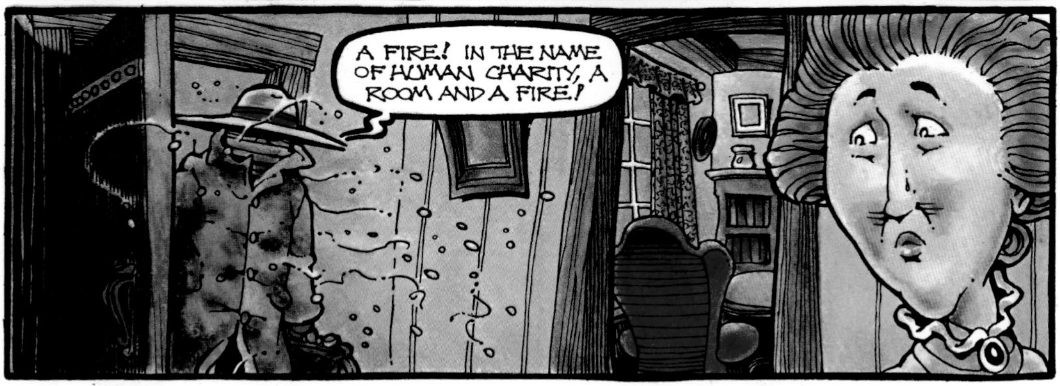
A FIRE! IN THE NAME OF HUMAN CHARITY, A ROOM AND A FIRE!

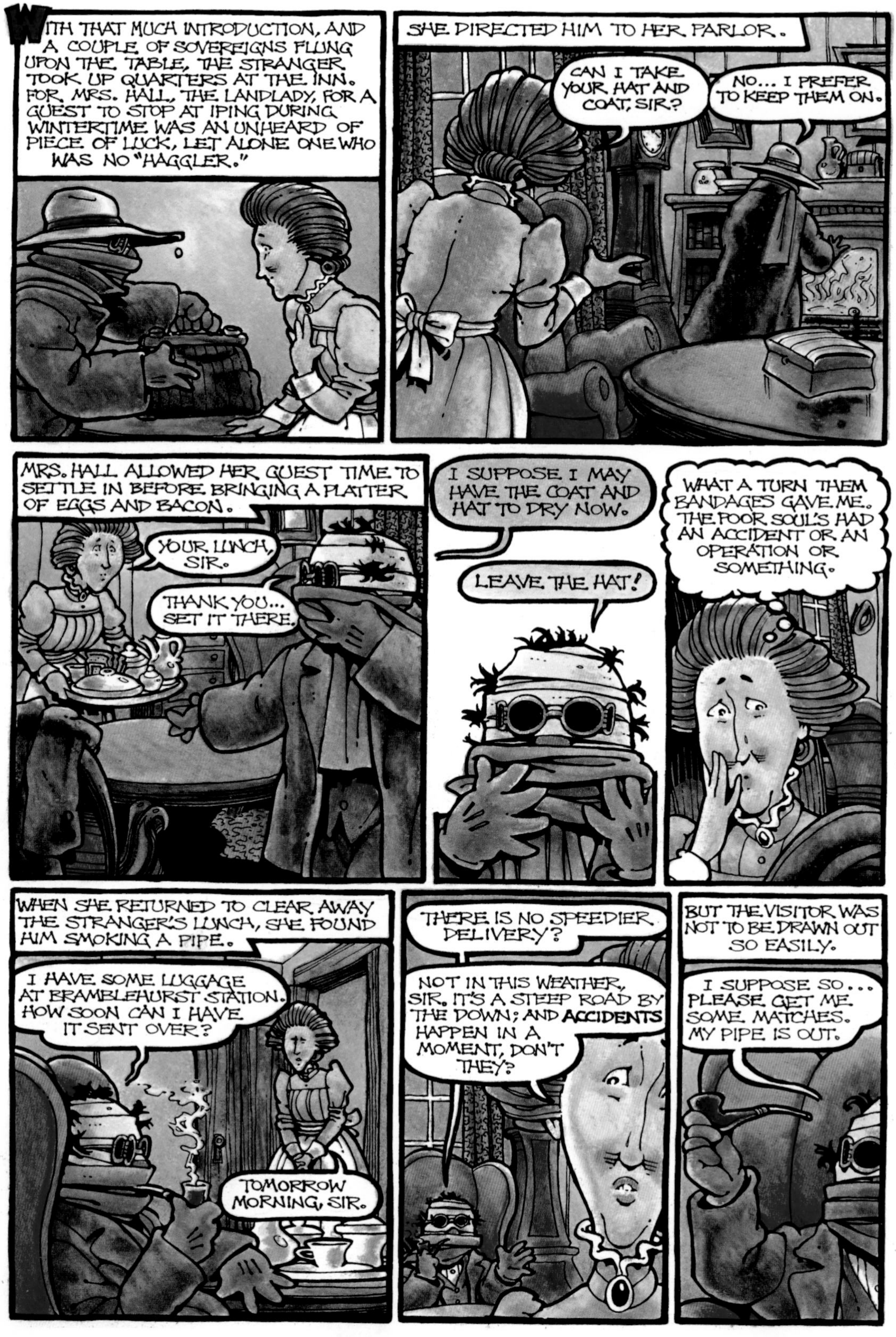
WITH THAT MUCH INTRODUCTION, AND A COUPLE OF SOVEREIGNS FLUNG UPON THE TABLE, THE STRANGER TOOK UP QUARTERS AT THE INN. FOR MRS. HALL, THE LANDLADY, FOR A GUEST TO STOP AT IPING DURING WINTERTIME WAS AN UNHEARD OF PIECE OF LUCK, LET ALONE ONE WHO WAS NO "HAGGLER."
SHE DIRECTED HIM TO HER PARLOR.
CAN I TAKE YOUR HAT AND COAT, SIR?
NO... I PREFER TO KEEP THEM ON.
MRS. HALL ALLOWED HER GUEST TIME TO SETTLE IN BEFORE BRINGING A PLATTER OF EGGS AND BACON.
YOUR LUNCH, SIR.
THANK YOU... SET IT THERE.
I SUPPOSE I MAY HAVE THE COAT AND HAT TO DRY NOW.
LEAVE THE HAT!
WHAT A TURN THEM BANDAGES GAVE ME. THE POOR SOUL'S HAD AN ACCIDENT OR AN OPERATION OR SOMETHING.
WHEN SHE RETURNED TO CLEAR AWAY THE STRANGER'S LUNCH, SHE FOUND HIM SMOKING A PIPE.
I HAVE SOME LUGGAGE AT BRAMBLEHURST STATION. HOW SOON CAN I HAVE IT SENT OVER?
TOMORROW MORNING, SIR.
THERE IS NO SPEEDIER DELIVERY?
NOT IN THIS WEATHER, SIR. IT'S A STEEP ROAD BY THE DOWN; AND ACCIDENTS HAPPEN IN A MOMENT, DON'T THEY?
BUT THE VISITOR WAS NOT TO BE DRAWN OUT SO EASILY.
I SUPPOSE SO... PLEASE GET ME SOME MATCHES. MY PIPE IS OUT.

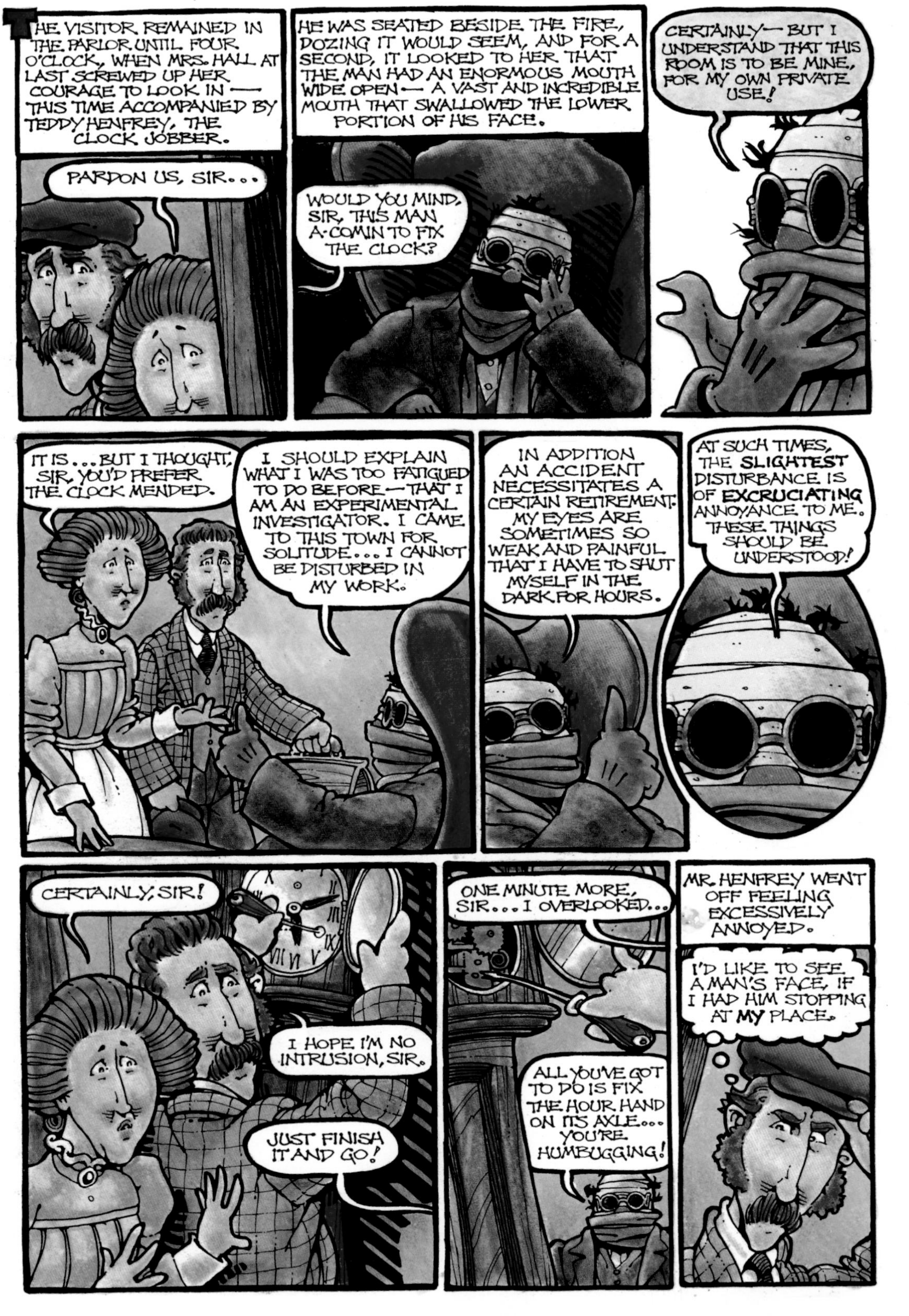
THE VISITOR REMAINED IN THE PARLOR UNTIL FOUR O'CLOCK, WHEN MRS. HALL AT LAST SCREWED UP HER COURAGE TO LOOK IN — THIS TIME ACCOMPANIED BY TEDDY HENFREY, THE CLOCK JOBBER.
PARDON US, SIR...
HE WAS SEATED BESIDE THE FIRE, DOZING IT WOULD SEEM, AND FOR A SECOND, IT LOOKED TO HER THAT THE MAN HAD AN ENORMOUS MOUTH WIDE OPEN — A VAST AND INCREDIBLE MOUTH THAT SWALLOWED THE LOWER PORTION OF HIS FACE.
WOULD YOU MIND, SIR, THIS MAN A-COMIN TO FIX THE CLOCK?
CERTAINLY — BUT I UNDERSTAND THAT THIS ROOM IS TO BE MINE, FOR MY OWN PRIVATE USE!
IT IS... BUT I THOUGHT, SIR, YOU'D PREFER THE CLOCK MENDED.
I SHOULD EXPLAIN WHAT I WAS TOO FATIGUED TO DO BEFORE — THAT I AM AN EXPERIMENTAL INVESTIGATOR. I CAME TO THIS TOWN FOR SOLITUDE... I CANNOT BE DISTURBED IN MY WORK.
IN ADDITION AN ACCIDENT NECESSITATES A CERTAIN RETIREMENT. MY EYES ARE SOMETIMES SO WEAK AND PAINFUL THAT I HAVE TO SHUT MYSELF IN THE DARK FOR HOURS.
AT SUCH TIMES, THE SLIGHTEST DISTURBANCE IS OF EXCRUCIATING ANNOYANCE TO ME. THESE THINGS SHOULD BE UNDERSTOOD!
CERTAINLY, SIR!
I HOPE I'M NO INTRUSION, SIR.
JUST FINISH IT AND GO!
ONE MINUTE MORE, SIR... I OVERLOOKED...
ALL YOU'VE GOT TO DO IS FIX THE HOUR HAND ON ITS AXLE... YOU'RE HUMBUGGING!
MR. HENFREY WENT OFF FEELING EXCESSIVELY ANNOYED.
I'D LIKE TO SEE A MAN'S FACE, IF I HAD HIM STOPPING AT MY PLACE.

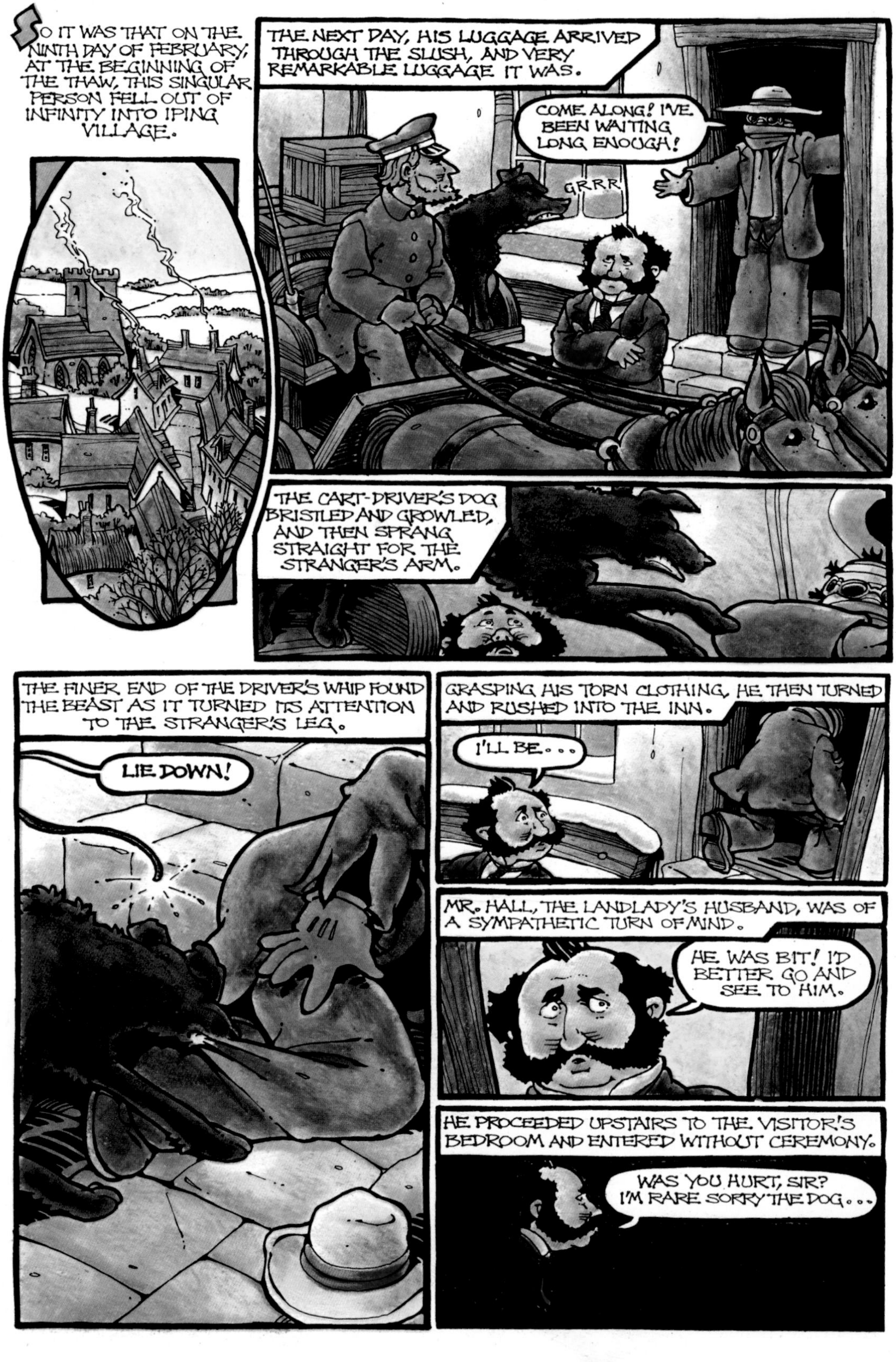
SO IT WAS THAT ON THE NINTH DAY OF FEBRUARY, AT THE BEGINNING OF THE THAW, THIS SINGULAR PERSON FELL OUT OF INFINITY INTO IPING VILLAGE.
THE NEXT DAY, HIS LUGGAGE ARRIVED THROUGH THE SLUSH, AND VERY REMARKABLE LUGGAGE IT WAS.
COME ALONG! I'VE BEEN WAITING LONG ENOUGH!
GRRR
THE CART-DRIVER'S DOG BRISTLED AND GROWLED, AND THEN SPRANG STRAIGHT FOR THE STRANGER'S ARM.
THE FINER END OF THE DRIVER'S WHIP FOUND THE BEAST AS IT TURNED ITS ATTENTION TO THE STRANGER'S LEG.
LIE DOWN!
GRASPING HIS TORN CLOTHING, HE THEN TURNED AND RUSHED INTO THE INN.
I'LL BE...
MR. HALL, THE LANDLADY'S HUSBAND, WAS OF A SYMPATHETIC TURN OF MIND.
HE WAS BIT! I'D BETTER GO AND SEE TO HIM.
HE PROCEEDED UPSTAIRS TO THE VISITOR'S BEDROOM AND ENTERED WITHOUT CEREMONY.
WAS YOU HURT, SIR? I'M RARE SORRY THE DOG...

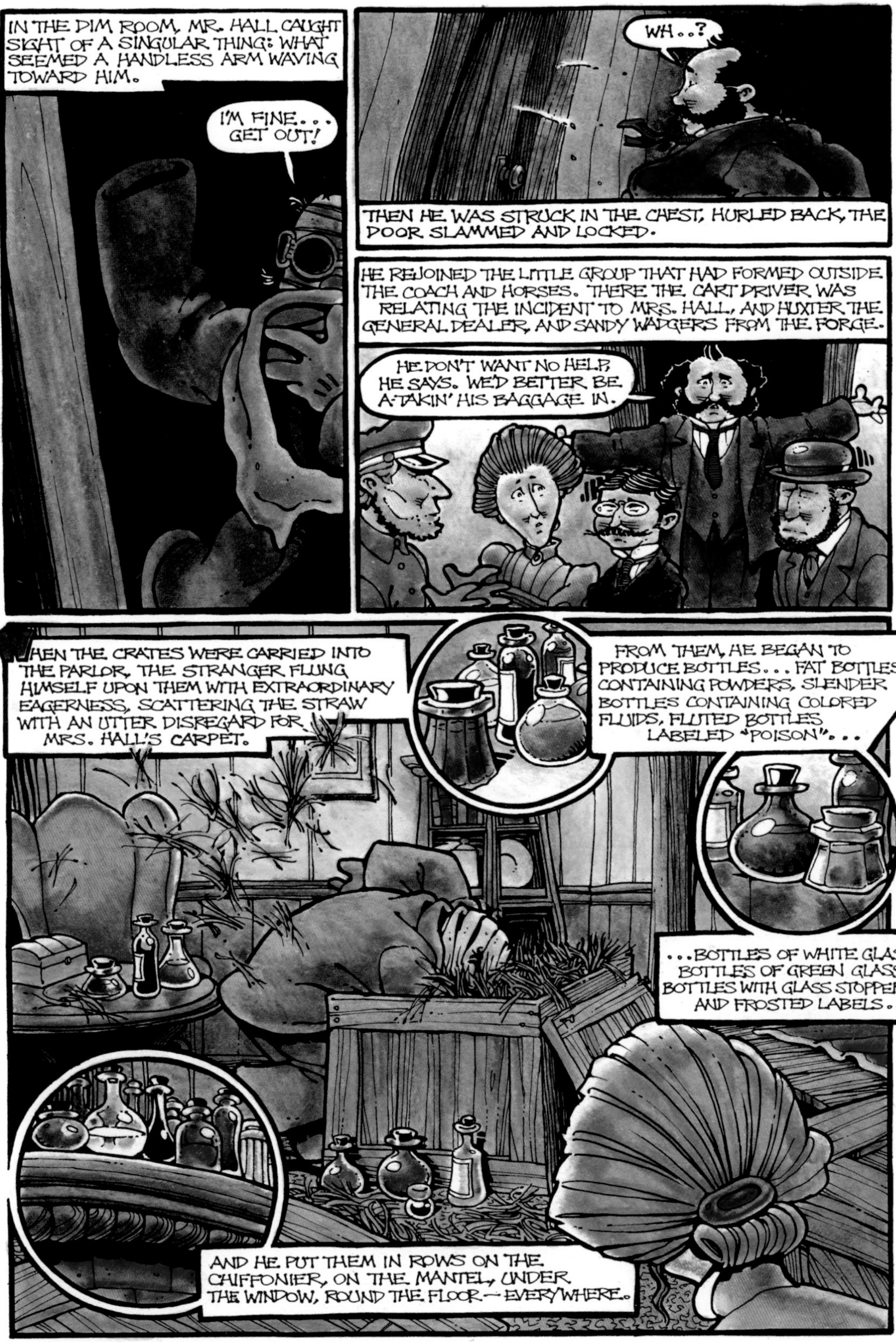
IN THE DIM ROOM, MR. HALL CAUGHT SIGHT OF A SINGULAR THING: WHAT SEEMED A HANDLESS ARM WAVING TOWARD HIM.
I'M FINE... GET OUT!
WH..?
THEN HE WAS STRUCK IN THE CHEST, HURLED BACK, THE DOOR SLAMMED AND LOCKED.
HE REJOINED THE LITTLE GROUP THAT HAD FORMED OUTSIDE THE COACH AND HORSES. THERE THE CART DRIVER WAS RELATING THE INCIDENT TO MRS. HALL, AND HUXTER THE GENERAL DEALER, AND SANDY WADGERS FROM THE FORGE.
HE DON'T WANT NO HELP, HE SAYS. WE'D BETTER BE A-TAKIN' HIS BAGGAGE IN.
WHEN THE CRATES WERE CARRIED INTO THE PARLOR, THE STRANGER FLUNG HIMSELF UPON THEM WITH EXTRAORDINARY EAGERNESS, SCATTERING THE STRAW WITH AN UTTER DISREGARD FOR MRS. HALL'S CARPET.
FROM THEM, HE BEGAN TO PRODUCE BOTTLES... FAT BOTTLES CONTAINING POWDERS, SLENDER BOTTLES CONTAINING COLORED FLUIDS, FLUTED BOTTLES LABELED "POISON"...
...BOTTLES OF WHITE GLASS, BOTTLES OF GREEN GLASS, BOTTLES WITH GLASS STOPPERS AND FROSTED LABELS...
AND HE PUT THEM IN ROWS ON THE CHIFFONIER, ON THE MANTEL, UNDER THE WINDOW, ROUND THE FLOOR — EVERYWHERE.

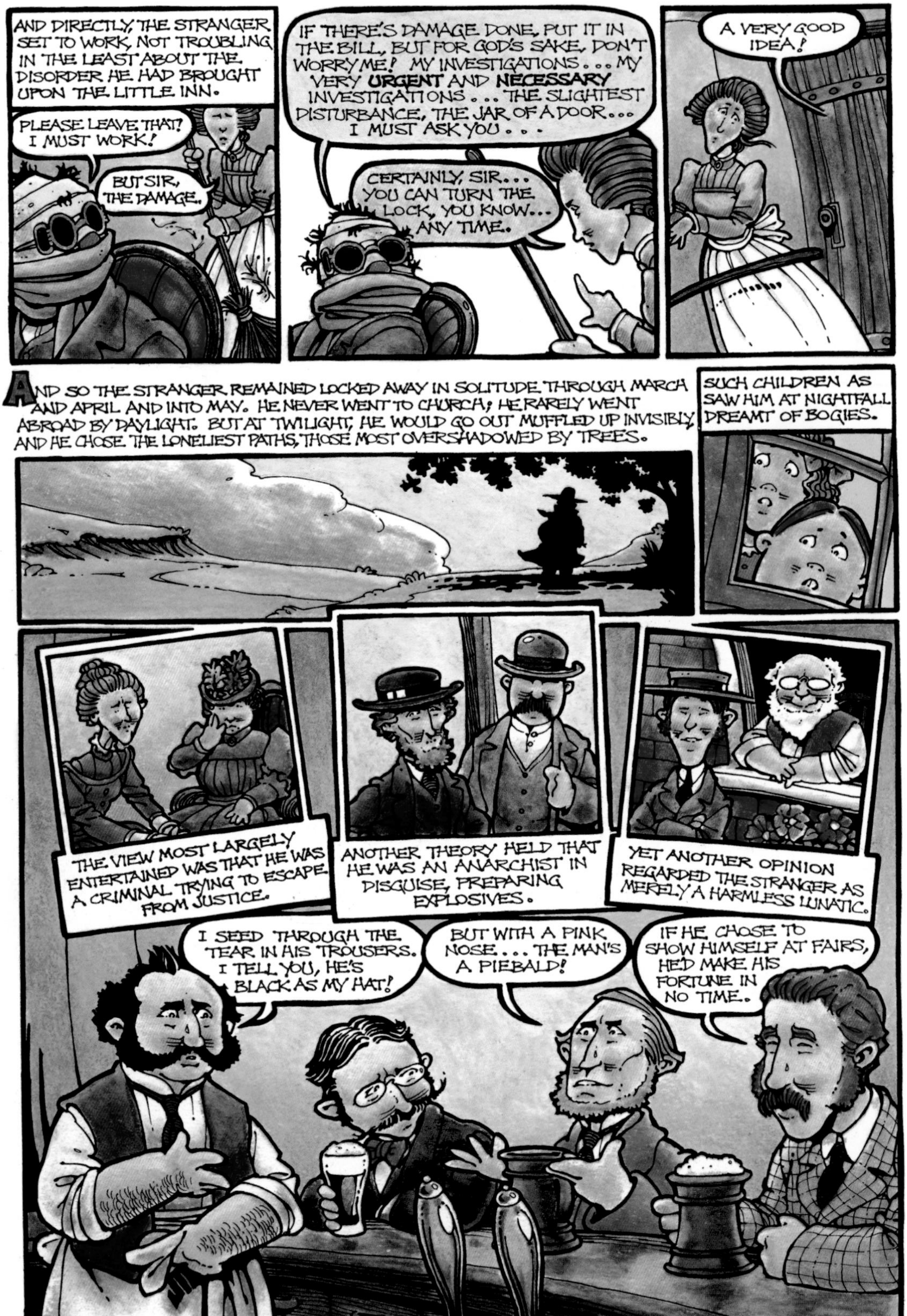
AND DIRECTLY, THE STRANGER SET TO WORK, NOT TROUBLING IN THE LEAST ABOUT THE DISORDER HE HAD BROUGHT UPON THE LITTLE INN.
PLEASE LEAVE THAT! I MUST WORK!
BUT SIR, THE DAMAGE.
IF THERE'S DAMAGE DONE, PUT IT IN THE BILL, BUT FOR GOD'S SAKE, DON'T WORRY ME! MY INVESTIGATIONS . . . MY VERY **URGENT** AND **NECESSARY** INVESTIGATIONS . . . THE SLIGHTEST DISTURBANCE, THE JAR OF A DOOR . . . I MUST ASK YOU . . .
CERTAINLY, SIR . . . YOU CAN TURN THE LOCK, YOU KNOW . . . ANY TIME.
A VERY GOOD IDEA!
AND SO THE STRANGER REMAINED LOCKED AWAY IN SOLITUDE THROUGH MARCH AND APRIL AND INTO MAY. HE NEVER WENT TO CHURCH; HE RARELY WENT ABROAD BY DAYLIGHT. BUT AT TWILIGHT, HE WOULD GO OUT MUFFLED UP INVISIBLY AND HE CHOSE THE LONELIEST PATHS, THOSE MOST OVERSHADOWED BY TREES.
SUCH CHILDREN AS SAW HIM AT NIGHTFALL DREAMT OF BOGIES.
THE VIEW MOST LARGELY ENTERTAINED WAS THAT HE WAS A CRIMINAL TRYING TO ESCAPE FROM JUSTICE.
ANOTHER THEORY HELD THAT HE WAS AN ANARCHIST IN DISGUISE, PREPARING EXPLOSIVES.
YET ANOTHER OPINION REGARDED THE STRANGER AS MERELY A HARMLESS LUNATIC.
I SEED THROUGH THE TEAR IN HIS TROUSERS. I TELL YOU, HE'S BLACK AS MY HAT!
BUT WITH A PINK NOSE . . . THE MAN'S A PIEBALD!
IF HE CHOSE TO SHOW HIMSELF AT FAIRS, HE'D MAKE HIS FORTUNE IN NO TIME.

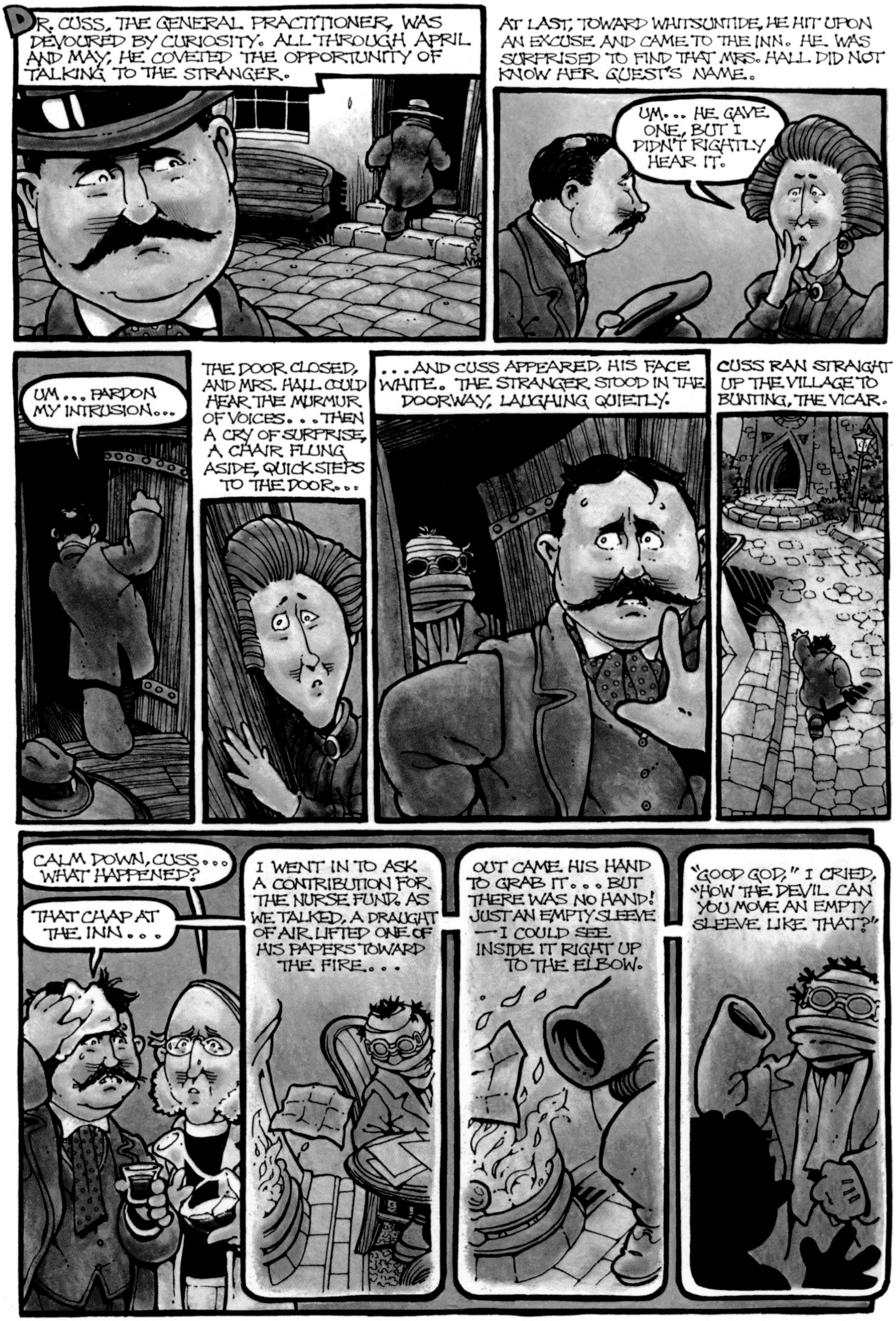
DR. CUSS, THE GENERAL PRACTITIONER, WAS DEVOURED BY CURIOSITY. ALL THROUGH APRIL AND MAY, HE COVETED THE OPPORTUNITY OF TALKING TO THE STRANGER.
AT LAST, TOWARD WHITSUNTIDE, HE HIT UPON AN EXCUSE AND CAME TO THE INN. HE WAS SURPRISED TO FIND THAT MRS. HALL DID NOT KNOW HER GUEST'S NAME.
UM... HE GAVE ONE, BUT I DIDN'T RIGHTLY HEAR IT.
UM... PARDON MY INTRUSION...
THE DOOR CLOSED, AND MRS. HALL COULD HEAR THE MURMUR OF VOICES... THEN A CRY OF SURPRISE, A CHAIR FLUNG ASIDE, QUICK STEPS TO THE DOOR...
...AND CUSS APPEARED, HIS FACE WHITE. THE STRANGER STOOD IN THE DOORWAY, LAUGHING QUIETLY.
CUSS RAN STRAIGHT UP THE VILLAGE TO BUNTING, THE VICAR.
CALM DOWN, CUSS... WHAT HAPPENED?
THAT CHAP AT THE INN...
I WENT IN TO ASK A CONTRIBUTION FOR THE NURSE FUND. AS WE TALKED, A DRAUGHT OF AIR LIFTED ONE OF HIS PAPERS TOWARD THE FIRE...
OUT CAME HIS HAND TO GRAB IT... BUT THERE WAS NO HAND! JUST AN EMPTY SLEEVE —I COULD SEE INSIDE IT RIGHT UP TO THE ELBOW.
"GOOD GOD," I CRIED, "HOW THE DEVIL CAN YOU MOVE AN EMPTY SLEEVE LIKE THAT?"

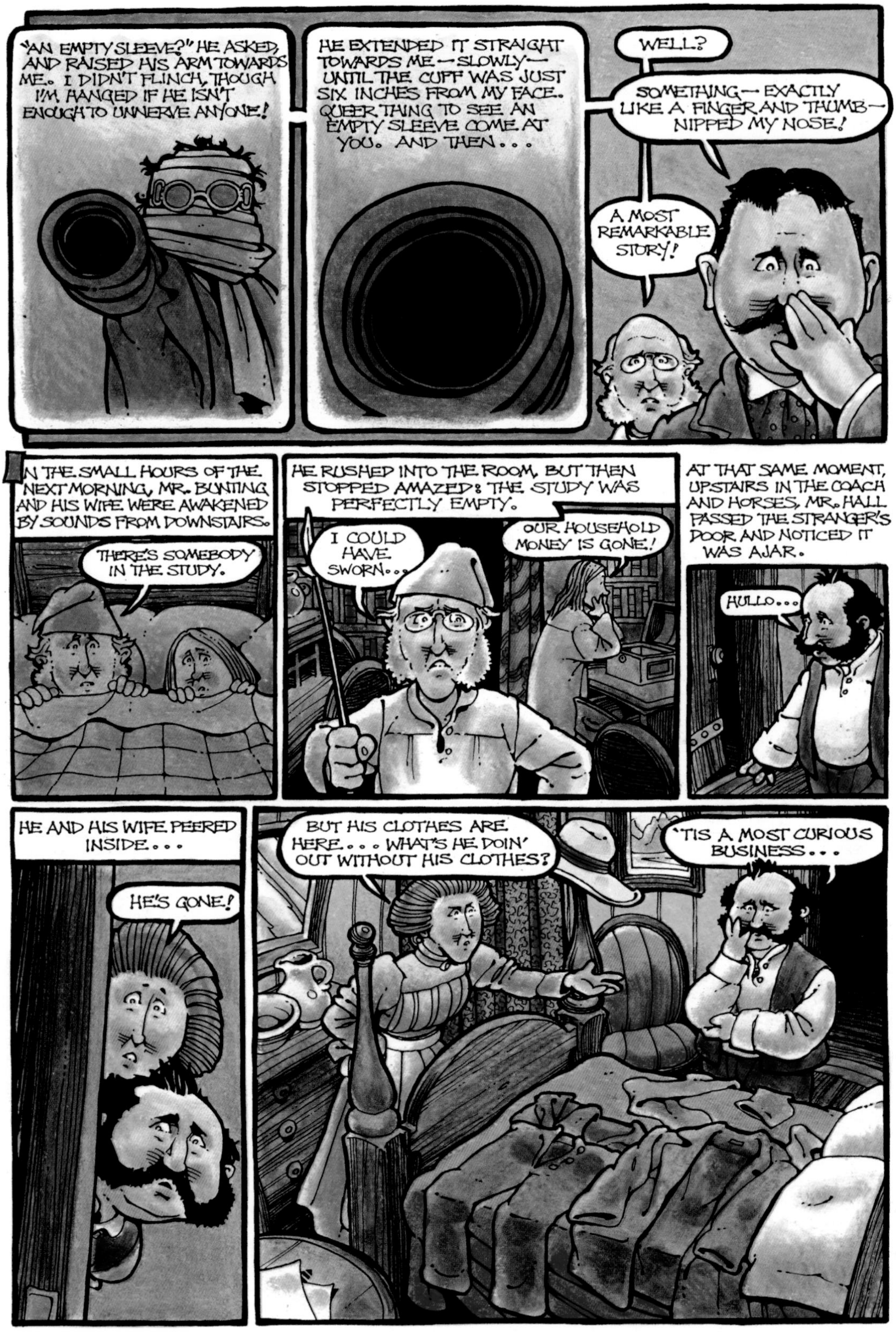
"AN EMPTY SLEEVE?" HE ASKED, AND RAISED HIS ARM TOWARDS ME. I DIDN'T FLINCH, THOUGH I'M HANGED IF HE ISN'T ENOUGH TO UNNERVE ANYONE!
HE EXTENDED IT STRAIGHT TOWARDS ME — SLOWLY — UNTIL THE CUFF WAS JUST SIX INCHES FROM MY FACE. QUEER THING TO SEE AN EMPTY SLEEVE COME AT YOU. AND THEN . . .
WELL?
SOMETHING — EXACTLY LIKE A FINGER AND THUMB — NIPPED MY NOSE!
A MOST REMARKABLE STORY!
IN THE SMALL HOURS OF THE NEXT MORNING, MR. BUNTING AND HIS WIFE WERE AWAKENED BY SOUNDS FROM DOWNSTAIRS.
THERE'S SOMEBODY IN THE STUDY.
HE RUSHED INTO THE ROOM, BUT THEN STOPPED AMAZED: THE STUDY WAS PERFECTLY EMPTY.
I COULD HAVE SWORN...
OUR HOUSEHOLD MONEY IS GONE!
AT THAT SAME MOMENT, UPSTAIRS IN THE COACH AND HORSES, MR. HALL PASSED THE STRANGER'S DOOR AND NOTICED IT WAS AJAR.
HULLO...
HE AND HIS WIFE PEERED INSIDE . . .
HE'S GONE!
BUT HIS CLOTHES ARE HERE . . . WHAT'S HE DOIN' OUT WITHOUT HIS CLOTHES?
'TIS A MOST CURIOUS BUSINESS . . .

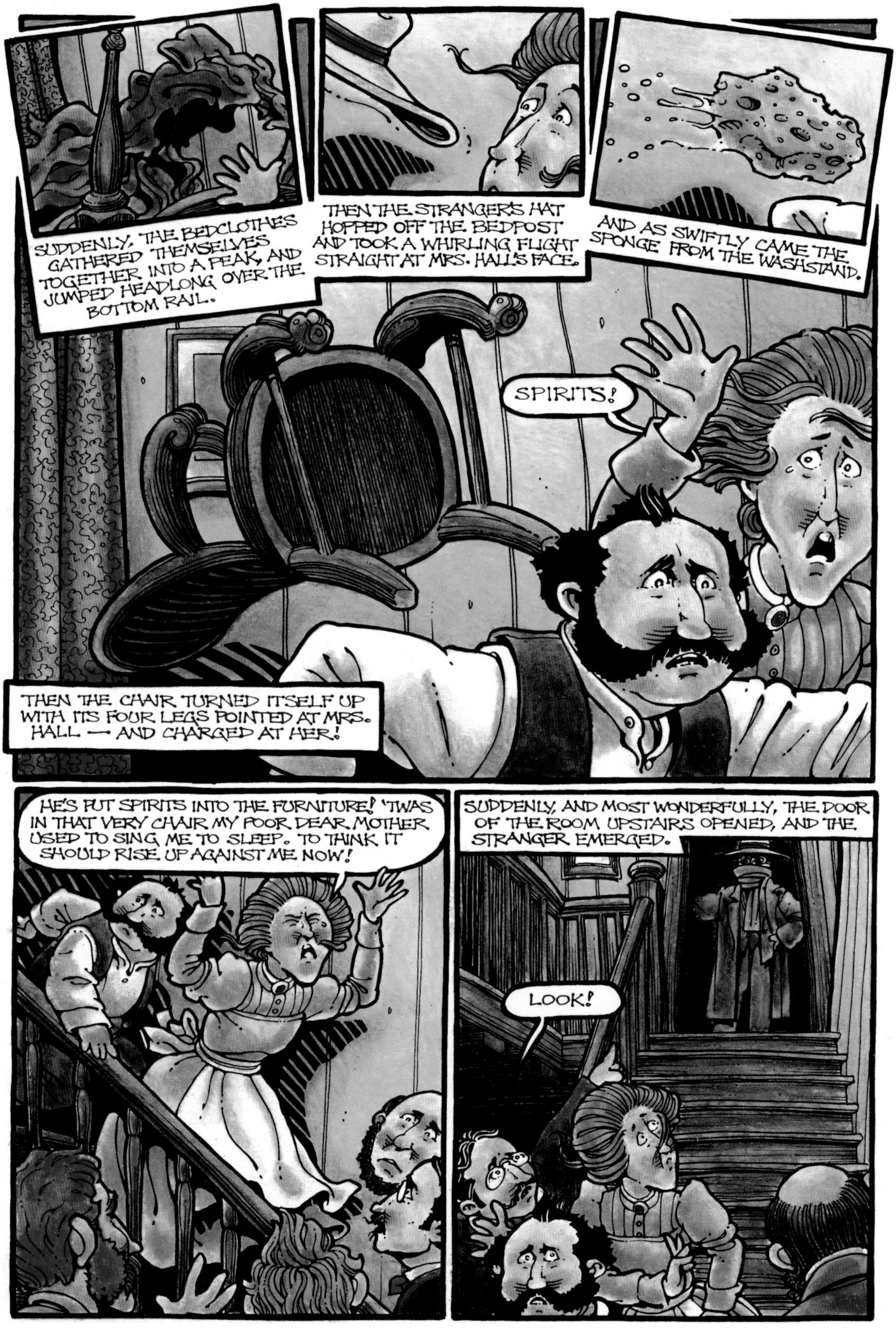
SUDDENLY, THE BEDCLOTHES GATHERED THEMSELVES TOGETHER INTO A PEAK, AND JUMPED HEADLONG OVER THE BOTTOM RAIL.
THEN THE STRANGER'S HAT HOPPED OFF THE BEDPOST AND TOOK A WHIRLING FLIGHT STRAIGHT AT MRS. HALL'S FACE.
AND AS SWIFTLY CAME THE SPONGE FROM THE WASHSTAND.
SPIRITS!
THEN THE CHAIR TURNED ITSELF UP WITH ITS FOUR LEGS POINTED AT MRS. HALL — AND CHARGED AT HER!
HE'S PUT SPIRITS INTO THE FURNITURE! 'TWAS IN THAT VERY CHAIR MY POOR DEAR MOTHER USED TO SING ME TO SLEEP. TO THINK IT SHOULD RISE UP AGAINST ME NOW!
SUDDENLY, AND MOST WONDERFULLY, THE DOOR OF THE ROOM UPSTAIRS OPENED, AND THE STRANGER EMERGED.
LOOK!

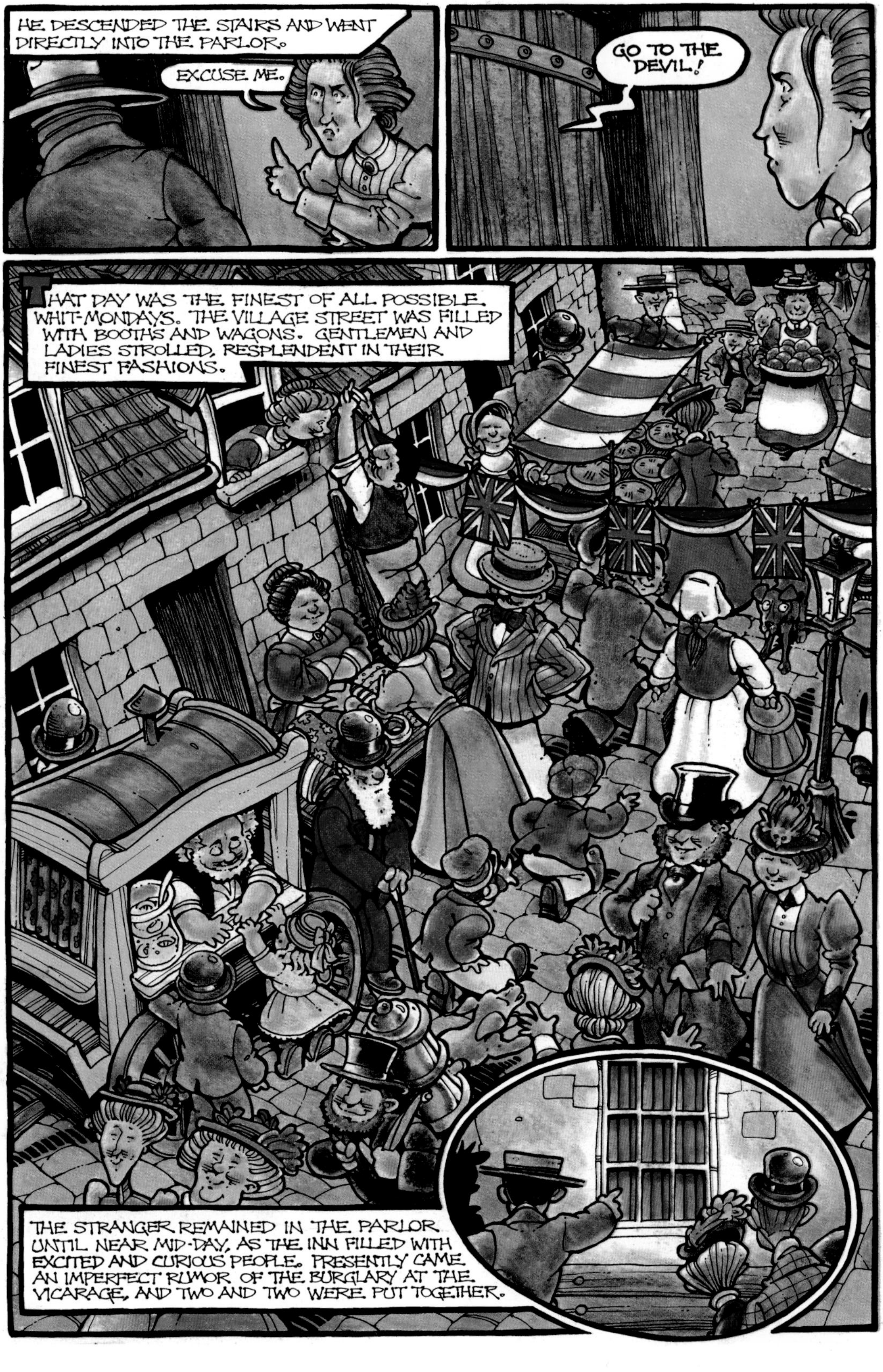
HE DESCENDED THE STAIRS AND WENT DIRECTLY INTO THE PARLOR.
EXCUSE ME.
GO TO THE DEVIL!
THAT DAY WAS THE FINEST OF ALL POSSIBLE WHIT-MONDAYS. THE VILLAGE STREET WAS FILLED WITH BOOTHS AND WAGONS. GENTLEMEN AND LADIES STROLLED, RESPLENDENT IN THEIR FINEST FASHIONS.
THE STRANGER REMAINED IN THE PARLOR UNTIL NEAR MID-DAY, AS THE INN FILLED WITH EXCITED AND CURIOUS PEOPLE. PRESENTLY CAME AN IMPERFECT RUMOR OF THE BURGLARY AT THE VICARAGE, AND TWO AND TWO WERE PUT TOGETHER.

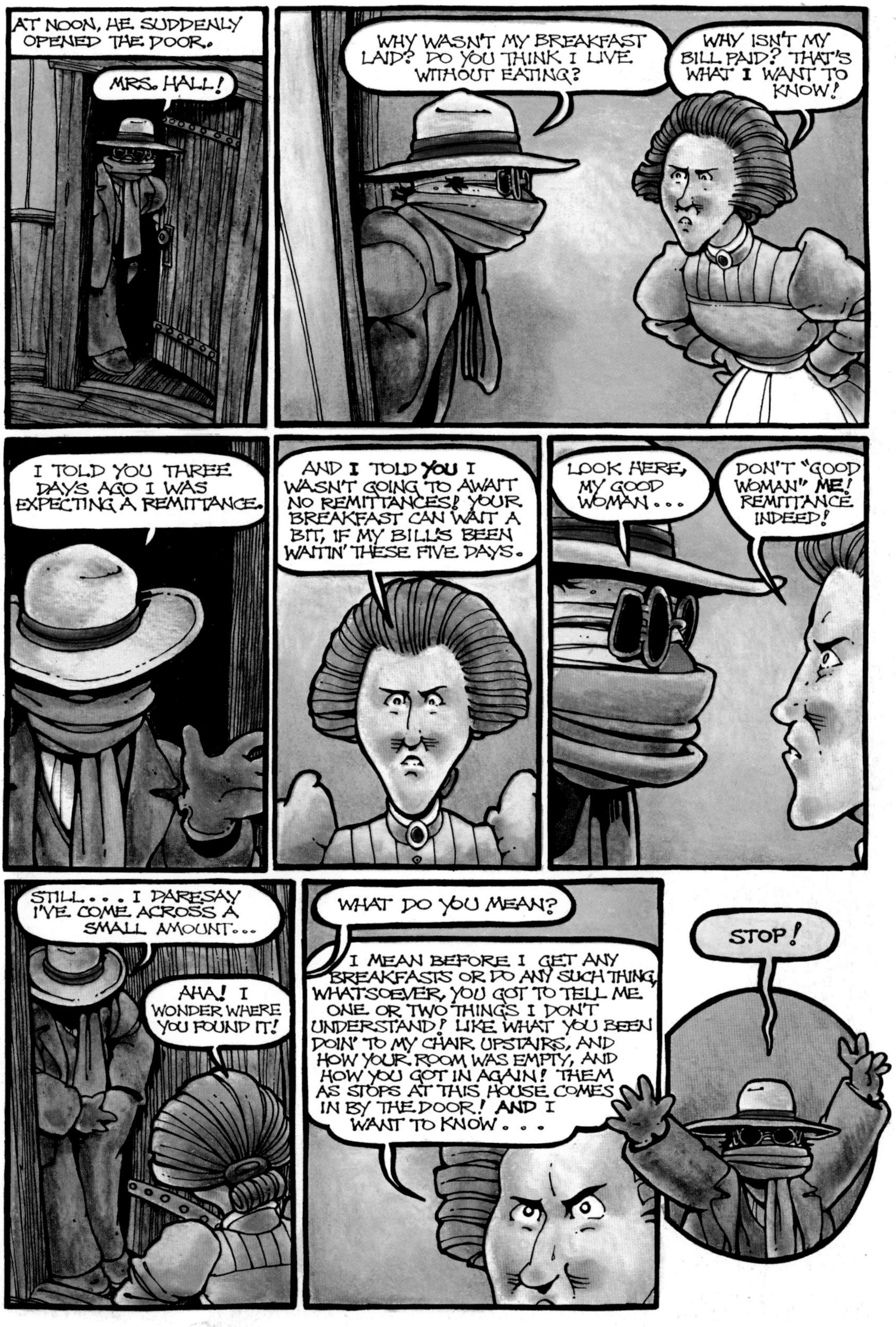

AT NOON, HE SUDDENLY OPENED THE DOOR.
MRS. HALL!
WHY WASN'T MY BREAKFAST LAID? DO YOU THINK I LIVE WITHOUT EATING?
WHY ISN'T MY BILL PAID? THAT'S WHAT I WANT TO KNOW!
I TOLD YOU THREE DAYS AGO I WAS EXPECTING A REMITTANCE.
AND I TOLD YOU I WASN'T GOING TO AWAIT NO REMITTANCES! YOUR BREAKFAST CAN WAIT A BIT, IF MY BILL'S BEEN WAITIN' THESE FIVE DAYS.
LOOK HERE, MY GOOD WOMAN...
DON'T "GOOD WOMAN" ME! REMITTANCE INDEED!
STILL... I DARESAY I'VE COME ACROSS A SMALL AMOUNT...
AHA! I WONDER WHERE YOU FOUND IT!
WHAT DO YOU MEAN?
I MEAN BEFORE I GET ANY BREAKFASTS OR DO ANY SUCH THING WHATSOEVER, YOU GOT TO TELL ME ONE OR TWO THINGS I DON'T UNDERSTAND! LIKE WHAT YOU BEEN DOIN' TO MY CHAIR UPSTAIRS, AND HOW YOUR ROOM WAS EMPTY, AND HOW YOU GOT IN AGAIN! THEM AS STOPS AT THIS HOUSE COMES IN BY THE DOOR! AND I WANT TO KNOW...
STOP!

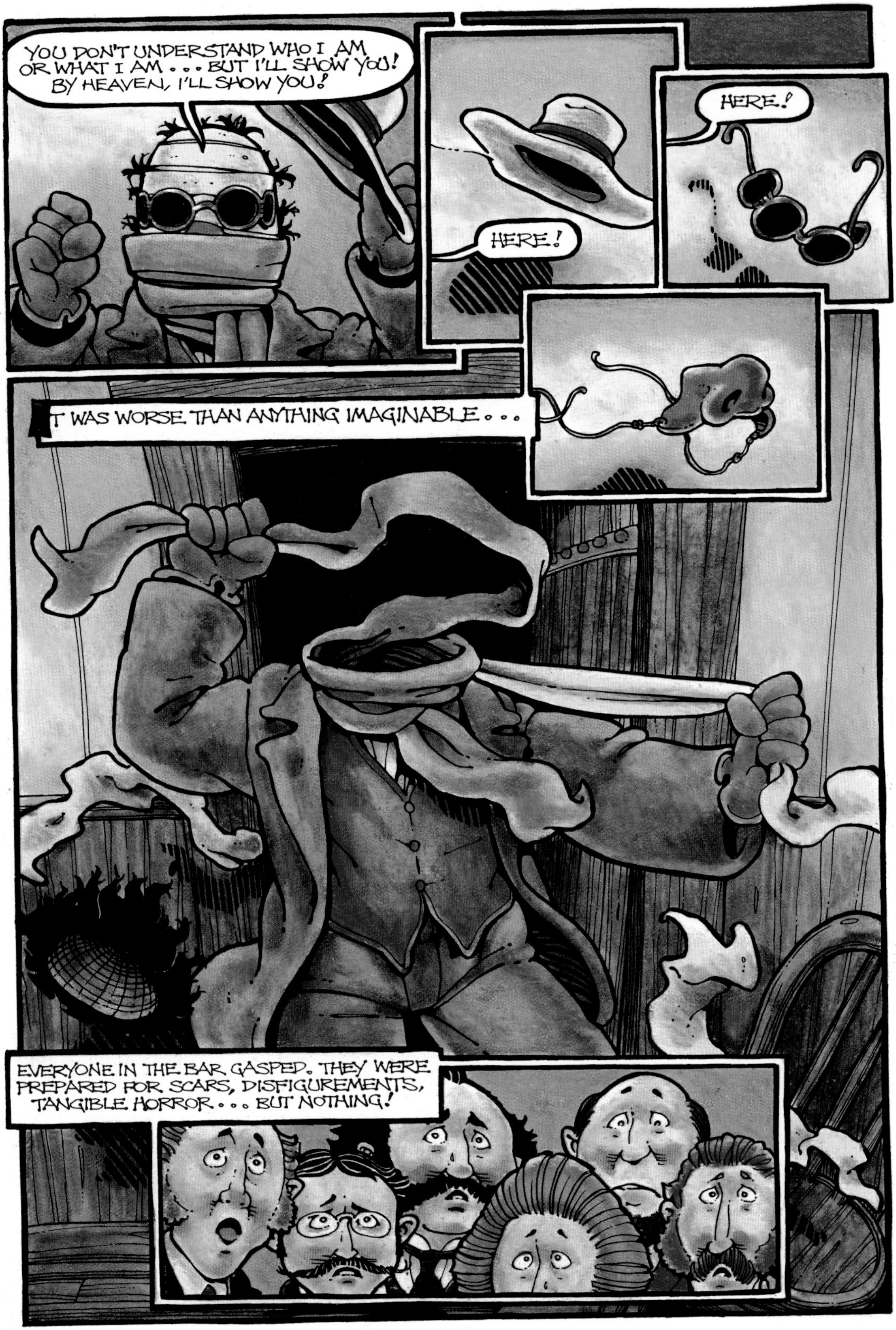
YOU DON'T UNDERSTAND WHO I AM OR WHAT I AM . . . BUT I'LL SHOW YOU! BY HEAVEN, I'LL SHOW YOU!
HERE!
HERE!
IT WAS WORSE THAN ANYTHING IMAGINABLE . . .
EVERYONE IN THE BAR GASPED. THEY WERE PREPARED FOR SCARS, DISFIGUREMENTS, TANGIBLE HORROR . . . BUT NOTHING!

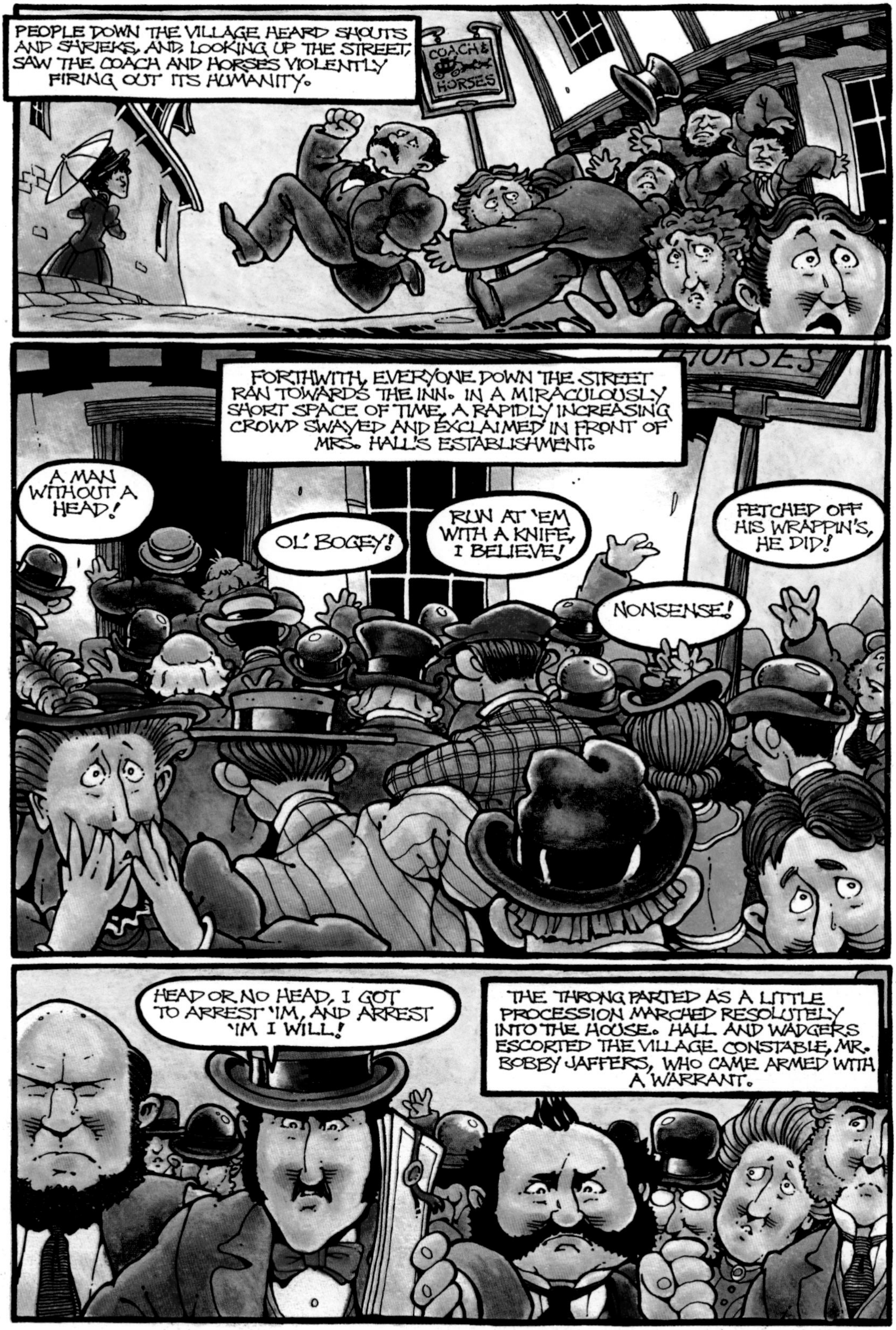
PEOPLE DOWN THE VILLAGE HEARD SHOUTS AND SHRIEKS, AND, LOOKING UP THE STREET, SAW THE COACH AND HORSES VIOLENTLY FIRING OUT ITS HUMANITY.
COACH & HORSES
FORTHWITH, EVERYONE DOWN THE STREET RAN TOWARDS THE INN. IN A MIRACULOUSLY SHORT SPACE OF TIME, A RAPIDLY INCREASING CROWD SWAYED AND EXCLAIMED IN FRONT OF MRS. HALL'S ESTABLISHMENT.
A MAN WITHOUT A HEAD!
OL' BOGEY!
RUN AT 'EM WITH A KNIFE, I BELIEVE!
FETCHED OFF HIS WRAPPIN'S, HE DID!
NONSENSE!
HEAD OR NO HEAD, I GOT TO ARREST 'IM, AND ARREST 'IM I WILL!
THE THRONG PARTED AS A LITTLE PROCESSION MARCHED RESOLUTELY INTO THE HOUSE. HALL AND WADGERS ESCORTED THE VILLAGE CONSTABLE, MR. BOBBY JAFFERS, WHO CAME ARMED WITH A WARRANT.

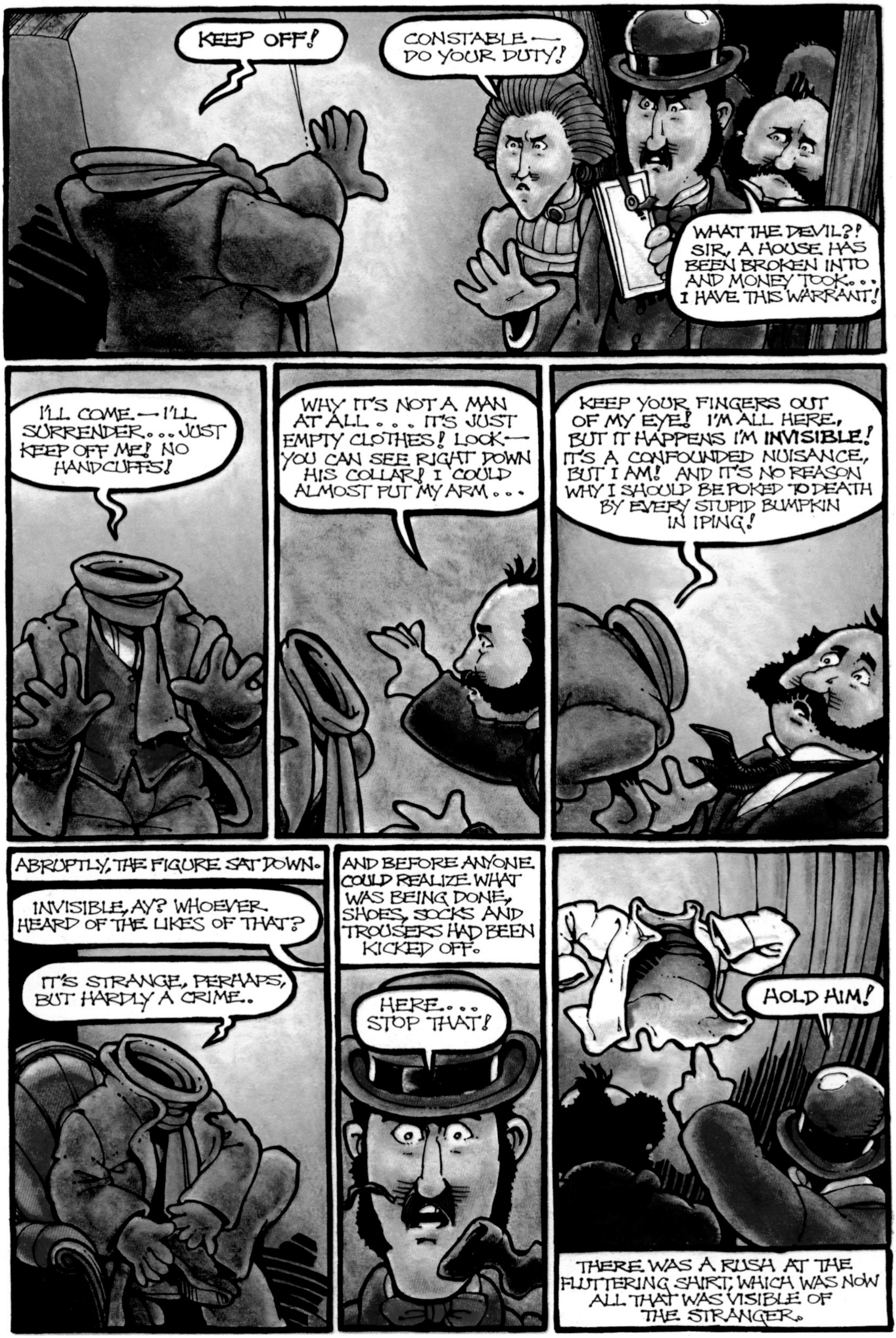
KEEP OFF!
CONSTABLE— DO YOUR DUTY!
WHAT THE DEVIL?! SIR, A HOUSE HAS BEEN BROKEN INTO AND MONEY TOOK... I HAVE THIS WARRANT!
I'LL COME—I'LL SURRENDER... JUST KEEP OFF ME! NO HANDCUFFS!
WHY IT'S NOT A MAN AT ALL... IT'S JUST EMPTY CLOTHES! LOOK— YOU CAN SEE RIGHT DOWN HIS COLLAR! I COULD ALMOST PUT MY ARM...
KEEP YOUR FINGERS OUT OF MY EYE! I'M ALL HERE, BUT IT HAPPENS I'M **INVISIBLE!** IT'S A CONFOUNDED NUISANCE, BUT I AM! AND IT'S NO REASON WHY I SHOULD BE POKED TO DEATH BY EVERY STUPID BUMPKIN IN IPING!
ABRUPTLY, THE FIGURE SAT DOWN.
INVISIBLE, AY? WHOEVER HEARD OF THE LIKES OF THAT?
IT'S STRANGE, PERHAPS, BUT HARDLY A CRIME.
AND BEFORE ANYONE COULD REALIZE WHAT WAS BEING DONE, SHOES, SOCKS AND TROUSERS HAD BEEN KICKED OFF.
HERE... STOP THAT!
HOLD HIM!
THERE WAS A RUSH AT THE FLUTTERING SHIRT, WHICH WAS NOW ALL THAT WAS VISIBLE OF THE STRANGER.

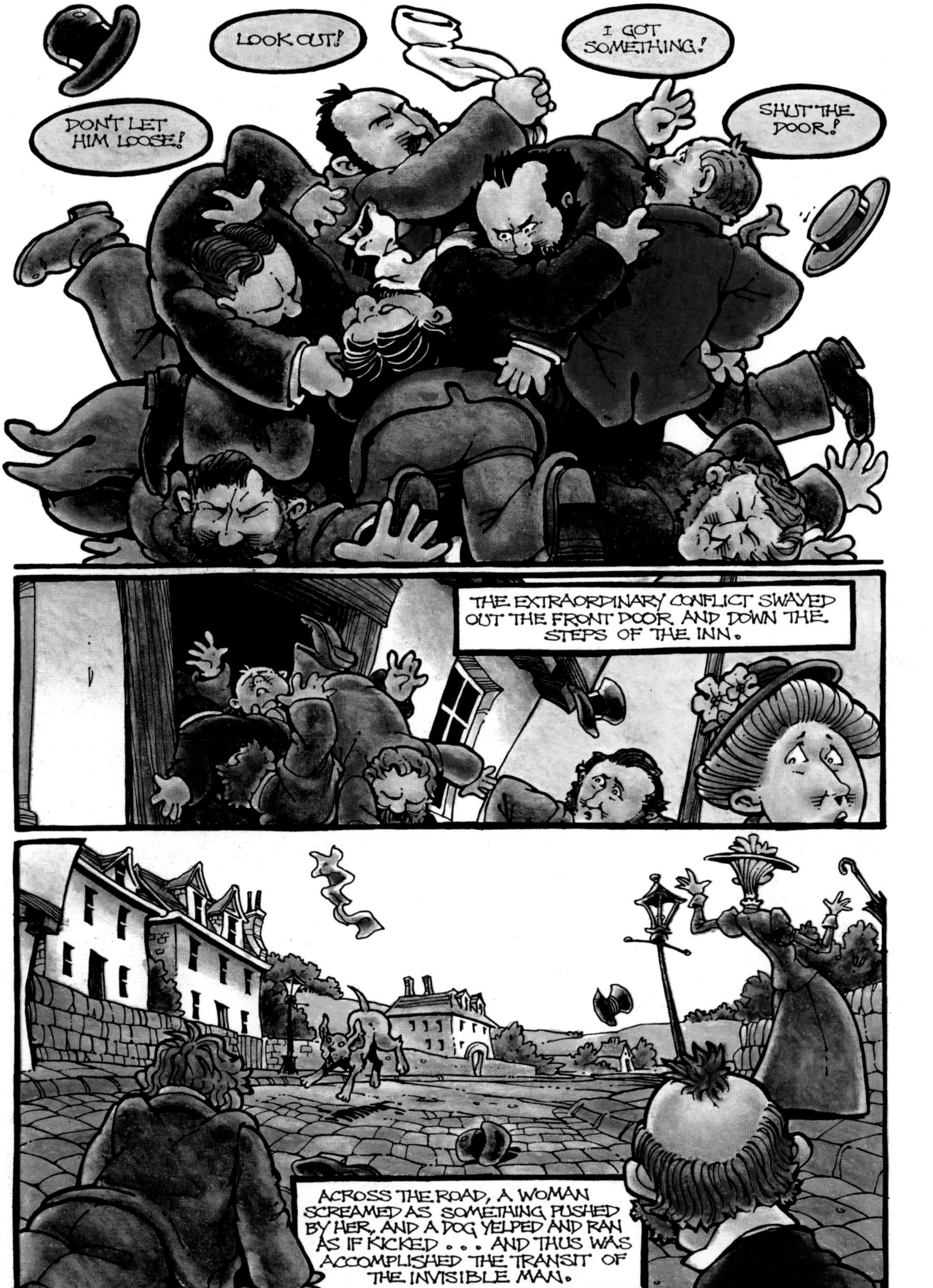
LOOK OUT!
I GOT SOMETHING!
DON'T LET HIM LOOSE!
SHUT THE DOOR!
THE EXTRAORDINARY CONFLICT SWAYED OUT THE FRONT DOOR AND DOWN THE STEPS OF THE INN.
ACROSS THE ROAD, A WOMAN SCREAMED AS SOMETHING PUSHED BY HER, AND A DOG YELPED AND RAN AS IF KICKED . . . AND THUS WAS ACCOMPLISHED THE TRANSIT OF THE INVISIBLE MAN.

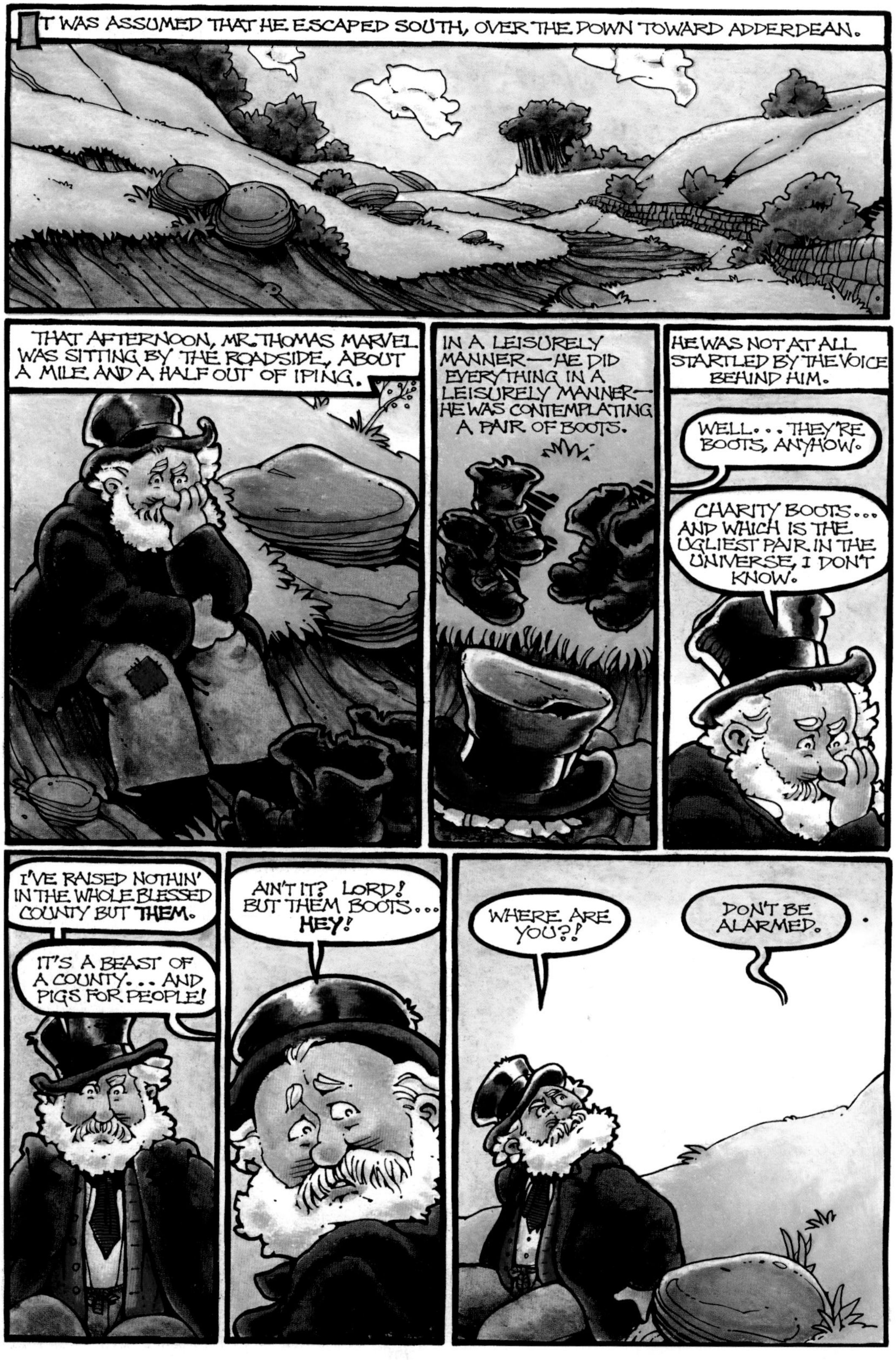
IT WAS ASSUMED THAT HE ESCAPED SOUTH, OVER THE DOWN TOWARD ADDERDEAN.
THAT AFTERNOON, MR. THOMAS MARVEL WAS SITTING BY THE ROADSIDE, ABOUT A MILE AND A HALF OUT OF IPING.
IN A LEISURELY MANNER—HE DID EVERYTHING IN A LEISURELY MANNER—HE WAS CONTEMPLATING A PAIR OF BOOTS.
HE WAS NOT AT ALL STARTLED BY THE VOICE BEHIND HIM.
WELL. . . THEY'RE BOOTS, ANYHOW.
CHARITY BOOTS... AND WHICH IS THE UGLIEST PAIR IN THE UNIVERSE, I DON'T KNOW.
I'VE RAISED NOTHIN' IN THE WHOLE BLESSED COUNTY BUT **THEM**.
IT'S A BEAST OF A COUNTY... AND PIGS FOR PEOPLE!
AIN'T IT? LORD! BUT THEM BOOTS... **HEY!**
WHERE ARE YOU?!
DON'T BE ALARMED.

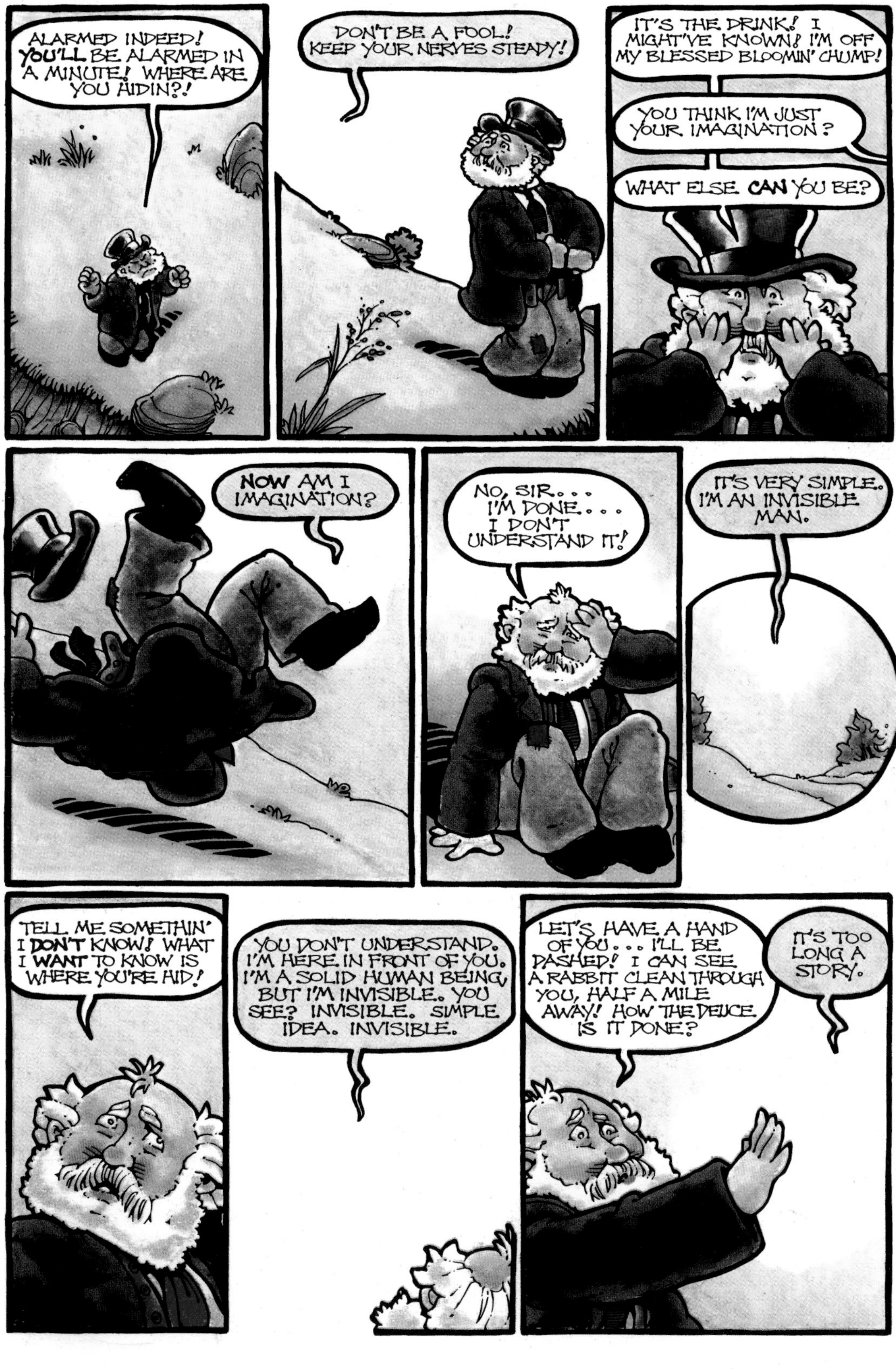

ALARMED INDEED! **YOU'LL** BE ALARMED IN A MINUTE! WHERE ARE YOU HIDIN?!
DON'T BE A FOOL! KEEP YOUR NERVES STEADY!
IT'S THE DRINK! I MIGHT'VE KNOWN! I'M OFF MY BLESSED BLOOMIN' CHUMP!
YOU THINK I'M JUST YOUR IMAGINATION?
WHAT ELSE **CAN** YOU BE?
NOW AM I IMAGINATION?
NO, SIR... I'M DONE... I DON'T UNDERSTAND IT!
IT'S VERY SIMPLE. I'M AN INVISIBLE MAN.
TELL ME SOMETHIN' I **DON'T** KNOW! WHAT I **WANT** TO KNOW IS WHERE YOU'RE HID!
YOU DON'T UNDERSTAND. I'M HERE IN FRONT OF YOU. I'M A SOLID HUMAN BEING, BUT I'M INVISIBLE. YOU SEE? INVISIBLE. SIMPLE IDEA. INVISIBLE.
LET'S HAVE A HAND OF YOU... I'LL BE DASHED! I CAN SEE A RABBIT CLEAN THROUGH YOU, HALF A MILE AWAY! HOW THE DEUCE IS IT DONE?
IT'S TOO LONG A STORY.

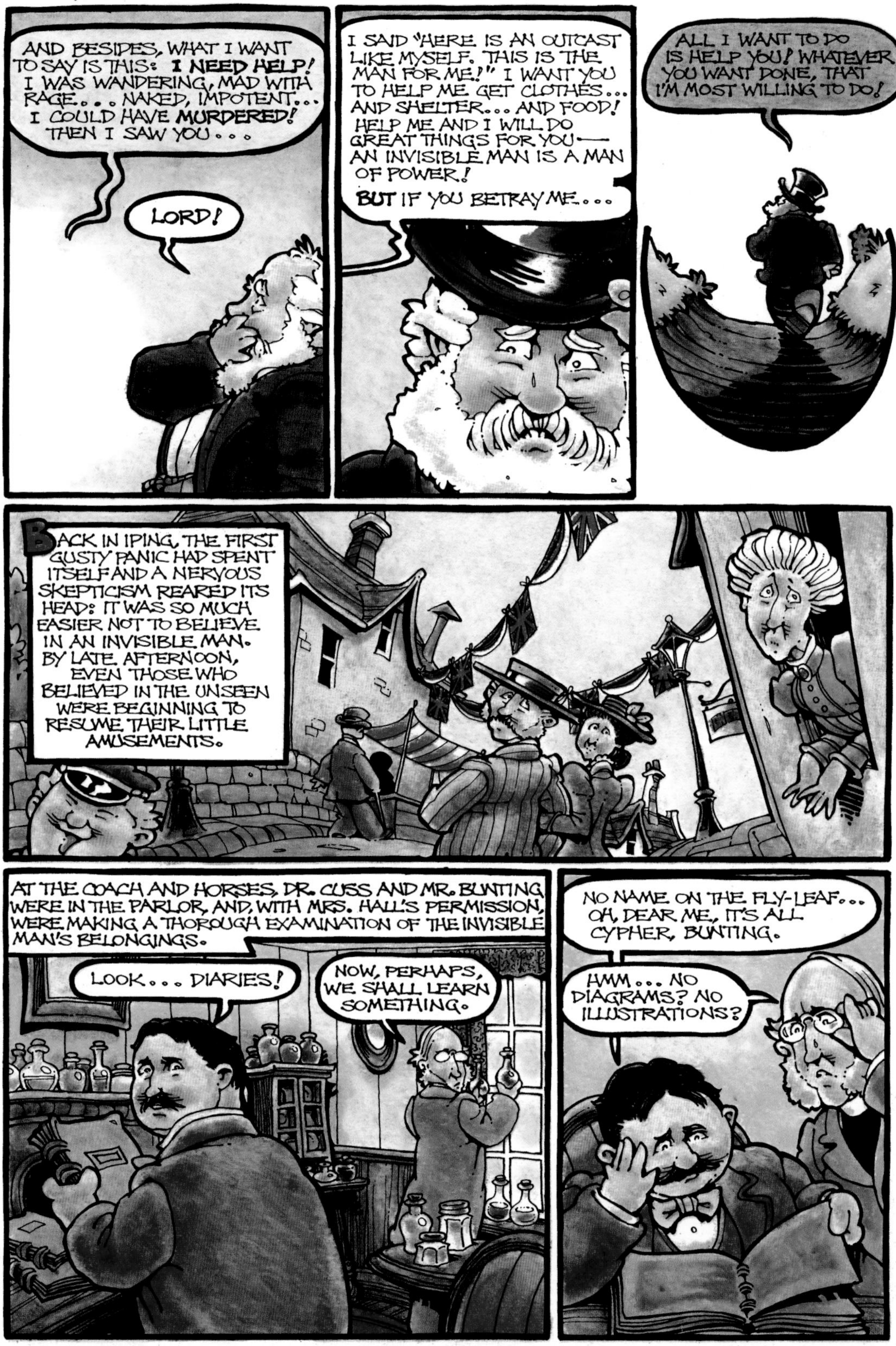
AND BESIDES, WHAT I WANT TO SAY IS THIS: I NEED HELP! I WAS WANDERING, MAD WITH RAGE... NAKED, IMPOTENT... I COULD HAVE MURDERED! THEN I SAW YOU...
LORD!
I SAID "HERE IS AN OUTCAST LIKE MYSELF. THIS IS THE MAN FOR ME!" I WANT YOU TO HELP ME GET CLOTHES... AND SHELTER... AND FOOD! HELP ME AND I WILL DO GREAT THINGS FOR YOU— AN INVISIBLE MAN IS A MAN OF POWER!
BUT IF YOU BETRAY ME...
ALL I WANT TO DO IS HELP YOU! WHATEVER YOU WANT DONE, THAT I'M MOST WILLING TO DO!
BACK IN IPING, THE FIRST GUSTY PANIC HAD SPENT ITSELF AND A NERVOUS SKEPTICISM REARED ITS HEAD: IT WAS SO MUCH EASIER NOT TO BELIEVE IN AN INVISIBLE MAN. BY LATE AFTERNOON, EVEN THOSE WHO BELIEVED IN THE UNSEEN WERE BEGINNING TO RESUME THEIR LITTLE AMUSEMENTS.
AT THE COACH AND HORSES, DR. CUSS AND MR. BUNTING WERE IN THE PARLOR, AND, WITH MRS. HALL'S PERMISSION, WERE MAKING A THOROUGH EXAMINATION OF THE INVISIBLE MAN'S BELONGINGS.
LOOK... DIARIES!
NOW, PERHAPS, WE SHALL LEARN SOMETHING.
NO NAME ON THE FLY-LEAF... OH, DEAR ME, IT'S ALL CYPHER, BUNTING.
HMM... NO DIAGRAMS? NO ILLUSTRATIONS?

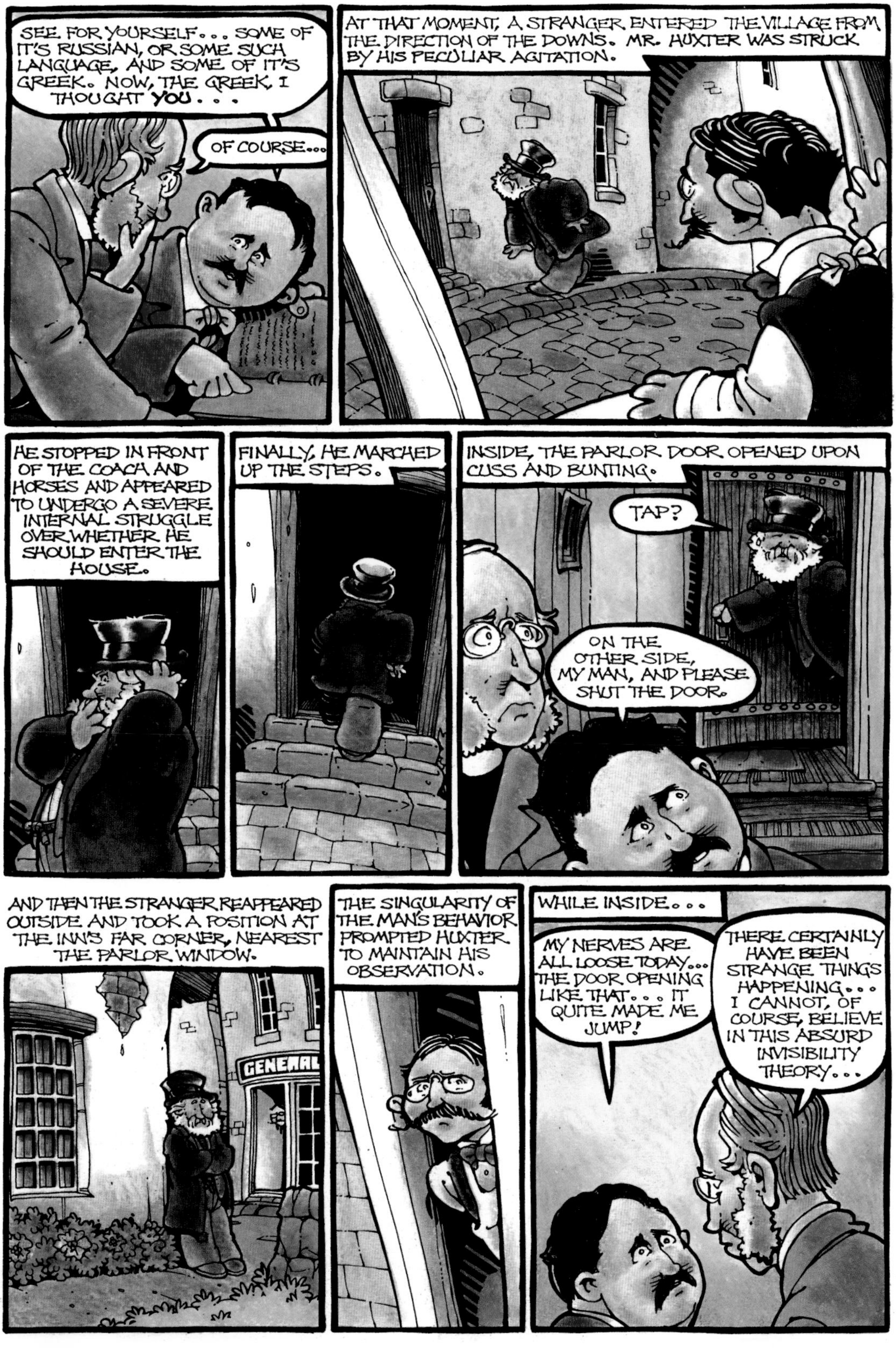
SEE FOR YOURSELF... SOME OF IT'S RUSSIAN, OR SOME SUCH LANGUAGE, AND SOME OF IT'S GREEK. NOW, THE GREEK, I THOUGHT **YOU**...
OF COURSE...
AT THAT MOMENT, A STRANGER ENTERED THE VILLAGE FROM THE DIRECTION OF THE DOWNS. MR. HUXTER WAS STRUCK BY HIS PECULIAR AGITATION.
HE STOPPED IN FRONT OF THE COACH AND HORSES AND APPEARED TO UNDERGO A SEVERE INTERNAL STRUGGLE OVER WHETHER HE SHOULD ENTER THE HOUSE.
FINALLY, HE MARCHED UP THE STEPS.
INSIDE, THE PARLOR DOOR OPENED UPON CUSS AND BUNTING.
TAP?
ON THE OTHER SIDE, MY MAN, AND PLEASE SHUT THE DOOR.
AND THEN THE STRANGER REAPPEARED OUTSIDE AND TOOK A POSITION AT THE INN'S FAR CORNER, NEAREST THE PARLOR WINDOW.
GENERAL
THE SINGULARITY OF THE MAN'S BEHAVIOR PROMPTED HUXTER TO MAINTAIN HIS OBSERVATION.
WHILE INSIDE...
MY NERVES ARE ALL LOOSE TODAY... THE DOOR OPENING LIKE THAT... IT QUITE MADE ME JUMP!
THERE CERTAINLY HAVE BEEN STRANGE THINGS HAPPENING... I CANNOT, OF COURSE, BELIEVE IN THIS ABSURD INVISIBILITY THEORY...

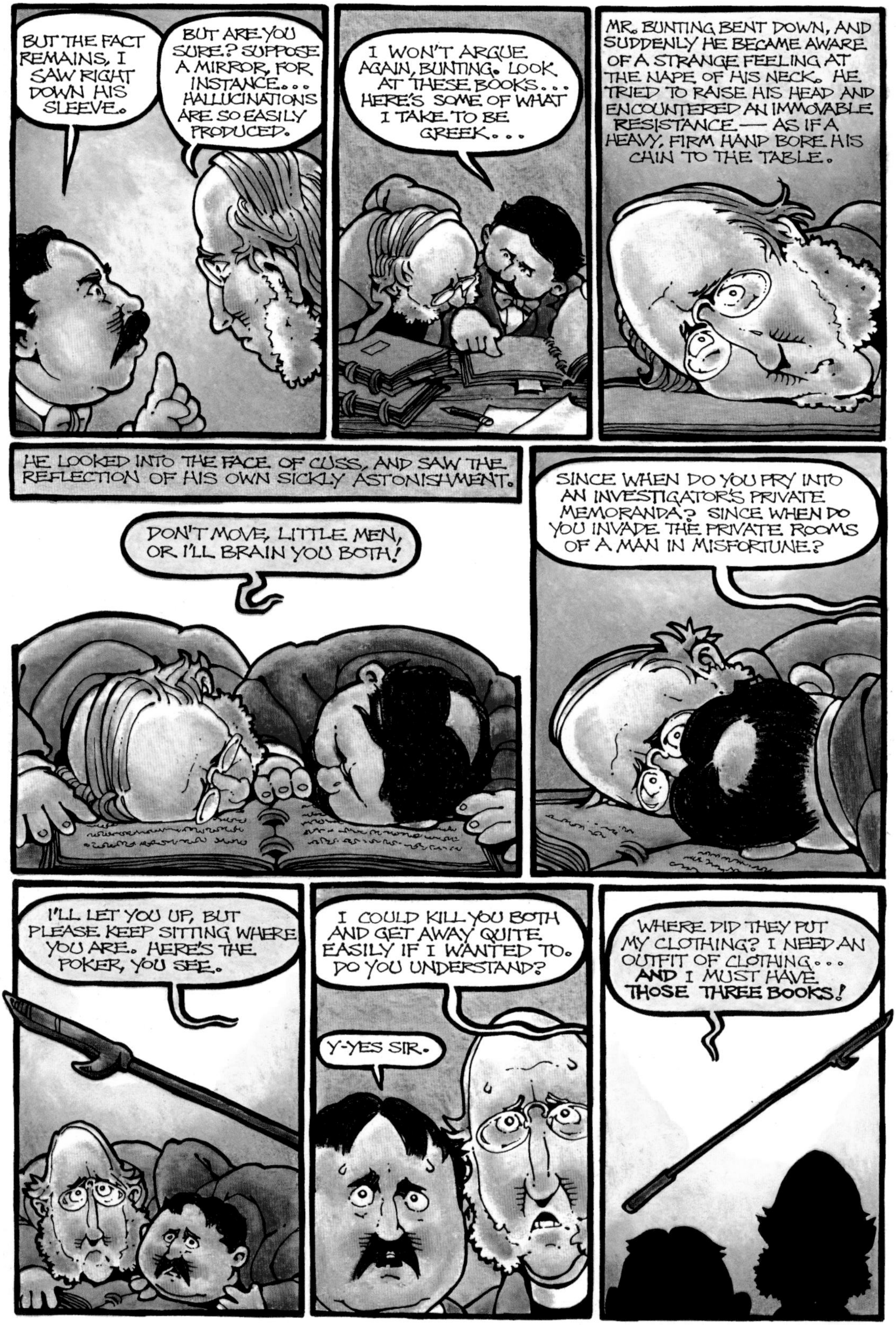
BUT THE FACT REMAINS, I SAW RIGHT DOWN HIS SLEEVE.
BUT ARE YOU SURE? SUPPOSE A MIRROR, FOR INSTANCE... HALLUCINATIONS ARE SO EASILY PRODUCED.
I WON'T ARGUE AGAIN, BUNTING. LOOK AT THESE BOOKS... HERE'S SOME OF WHAT I TAKE TO BE GREEK...
MR. BUNTING BENT DOWN, AND SUDDENLY HE BECAME AWARE OF A STRANGE FEELING AT THE NAPE OF HIS NECK. HE TRIED TO RAISE HIS HEAD AND ENCOUNTERED AN IMMOVABLE RESISTANCE — AS IF A HEAVY, FIRM HAND BORE HIS CHIN TO THE TABLE.
HE LOOKED INTO THE FACE OF CUSS, AND SAW THE REFLECTION OF HIS OWN SICKLY ASTONISHMENT.
DON'T MOVE, LITTLE MEN, OR I'LL BRAIN YOU BOTH!
SINCE WHEN DO YOU PRY INTO AN INVESTIGATOR'S PRIVATE MEMORANDA? SINCE WHEN DO YOU INVADE THE PRIVATE ROOMS OF A MAN IN MISFORTUNE?
I'LL LET YOU UP, BUT PLEASE KEEP SITTING WHERE YOU ARE. HERE'S THE POKER, YOU SEE.
I COULD KILL YOU BOTH AND GET AWAY QUITE EASILY IF I WANTED TO. DO YOU UNDERSTAND?
Y-YES SIR.
WHERE DID THEY PUT MY CLOTHING? I NEED AN OUTFIT OF CLOTHING... AND I MUST HAVE THOSE THREE BOOKS!

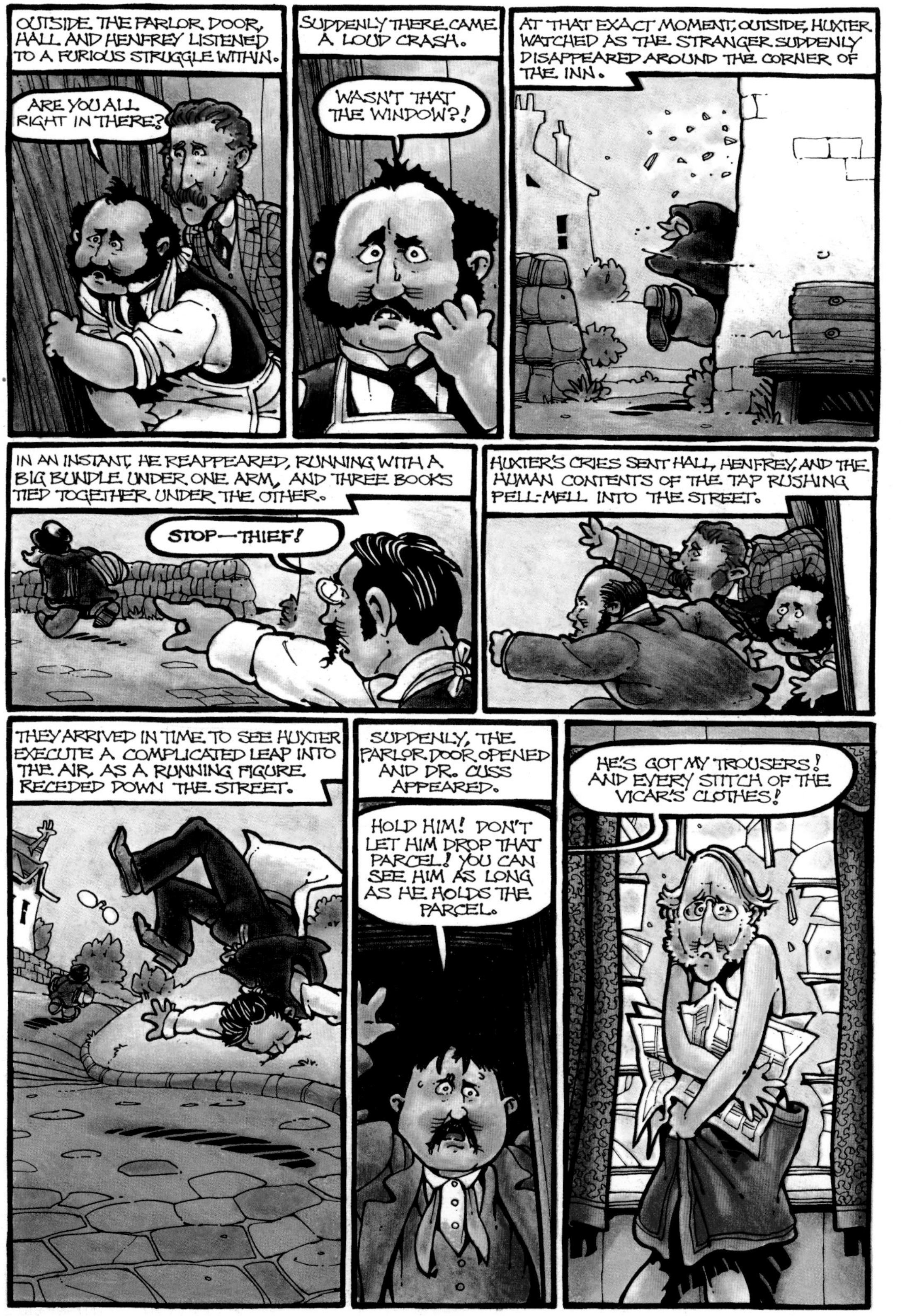

OUTSIDE THE PARLOR DOOR, HALL AND HENFREY LISTENED TO A FURIOUS STRUGGLE WITHIN.
ARE YOU ALL RIGHT IN THERE?
SUDDENLY THERE CAME A LOUD CRASH.
WASN'T THAT THE WINDOW?!
AT THAT EXACT MOMENT, OUTSIDE, HUXTER WATCHED AS THE STRANGER SUDDENLY DISAPPEARED AROUND THE CORNER OF THE INN.
IN AN INSTANT, HE REAPPEARED, RUNNING WITH A BIG BUNDLE UNDER ONE ARM, AND THREE BOOKS TIED TOGETHER UNDER THE OTHER.
STOP—THIEF!
HUXTER'S CRIES SENT HALL, HENFREY, AND THE HUMAN CONTENTS OF THE TAP RUSHING PELL-MELL INTO THE STREET.
THEY ARRIVED IN TIME TO SEE HUXTER EXECUTE A COMPLICATED LEAP INTO THE AIR, AS A RUNNING FIGURE RECEDED DOWN THE STREET.
SUDDENLY, THE PARLOR DOOR OPENED AND DR. CUSS APPEARED.
HOLD HIM! DON'T LET HIM DROP THAT PARCEL! YOU CAN SEE HIM AS LONG AS HE HOLDS THE PARCEL.
HE'S GOT MY TROUSERS! AND EVERY STITCH OF THE VICAR'S CLOTHES!

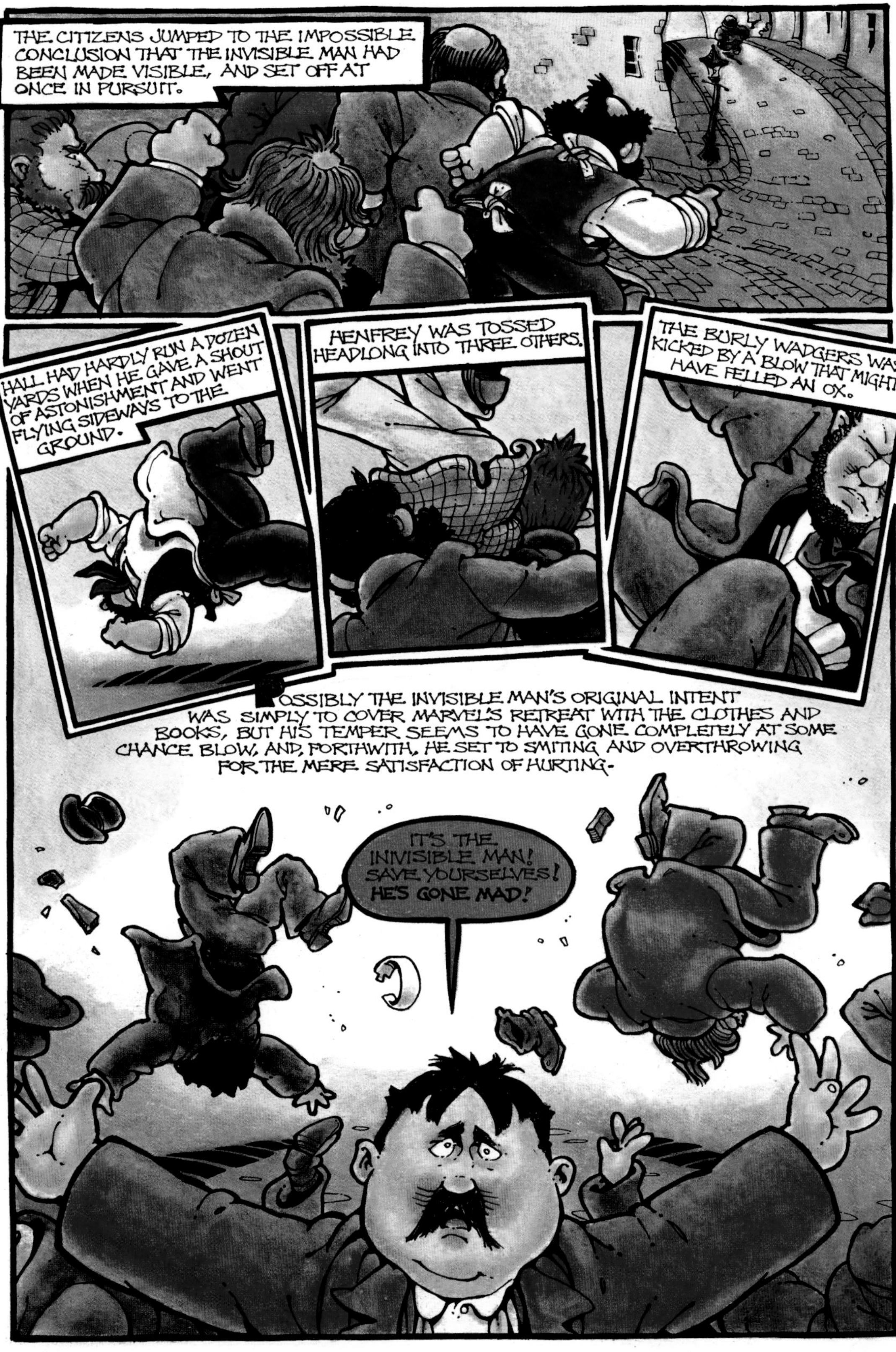
THE CITIZENS JUMPED TO THE IMPOSSIBLE CONCLUSION THAT THE INVISIBLE MAN HAD BEEN MADE VISIBLE, AND SET OFF AT ONCE IN PURSUIT.
HALL HAD HARDLY RUN A DOZEN YARDS WHEN HE GAVE A SHOUT OF ASTONISHMENT AND WENT FLYING SIDEWAYS TO THE GROUND.
HENFREY WAS TOSSED HEADLONG INTO THREE OTHERS.
THE BURLY WADGERS WAS KICKED BY A BLOW THAT MIGHT HAVE FELLED AN OX.
POSSIBLY THE INVISIBLE MAN'S ORIGINAL INTENT WAS SIMPLY TO COVER MARVEL'S RETREAT WITH THE CLOTHES AND BOOKS, BUT HIS TEMPER SEEMS TO HAVE GONE COMPLETELY AT SOME CHANCE BLOW, AND, FORTHWITH, HE SET TO SMITING AND OVERTHROWING FOR THE MERE SATISFACTION OF HURTING.
IT'S THE INVISIBLE MAN! SAVE YOURSELVES! HE'S GONE MAD!

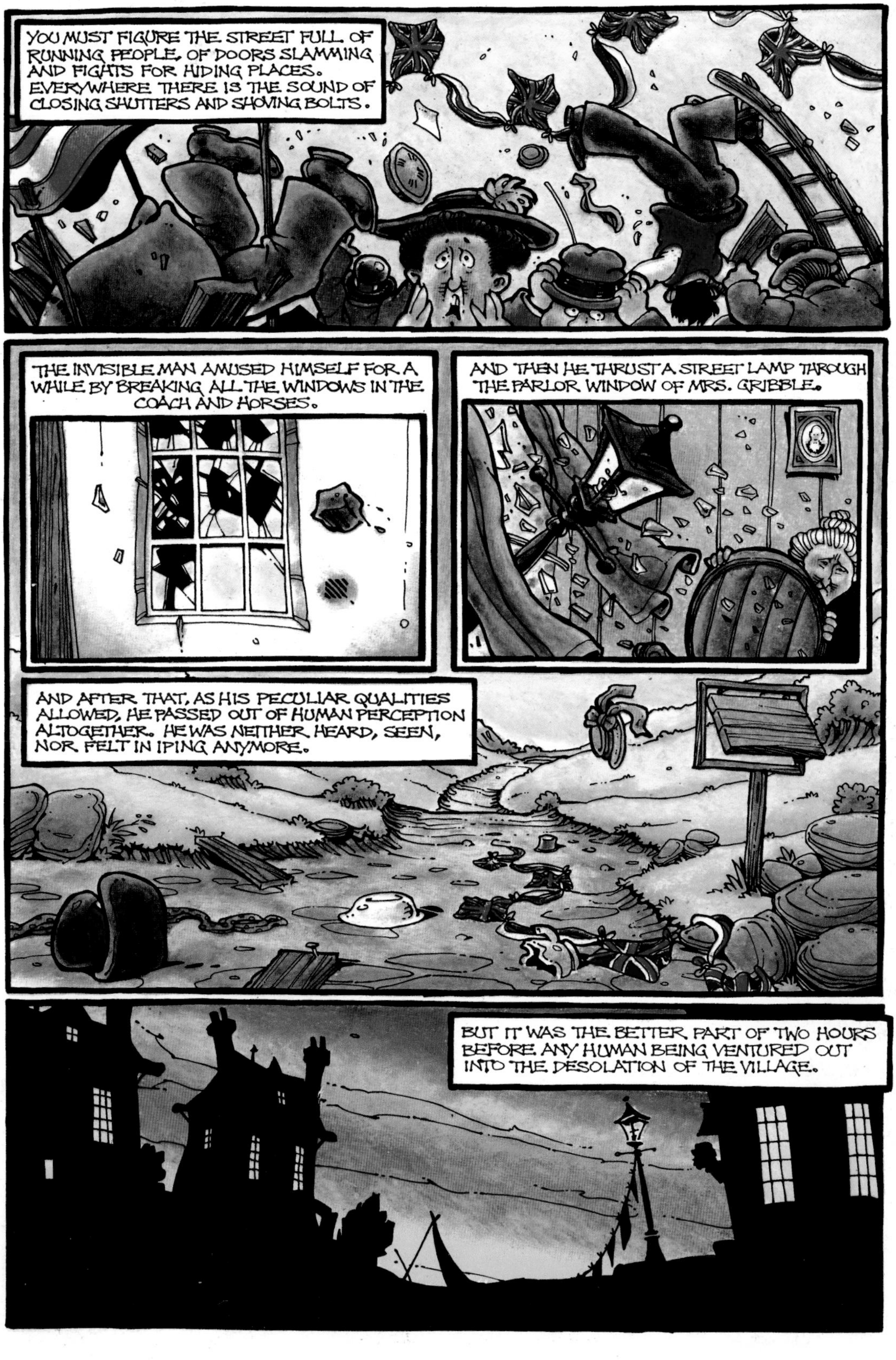
YOU MUST FIGURE THE STREET FULL OF RUNNING PEOPLE, OF DOORS SLAMMING AND FIGHTS FOR HIDING PLACES. EVERYWHERE THERE IS THE SOUND OF CLOSING SHUTTERS AND SHOVING BOLTS.
THE INVISIBLE MAN AMUSED HIMSELF FOR A WHILE BY BREAKING ALL THE WINDOWS IN THE COACH AND HORSES.
AND THEN HE THRUST A STREET LAMP THROUGH THE PARLOR WINDOW OF MRS. GRIBBLE.
AND AFTER THAT, AS HIS PECULIAR QUALITIES ALLOWED, HE PASSED OUT OF HUMAN PERCEPTION ALTOGETHER. HE WAS NEITHER HEARD, SEEN, NOR FELT IN IPING ANYMORE.
BUT IT WAS THE BETTER PART OF TWO HOURS BEFORE ANY HUMAN BEING VENTURED OUT INTO THE DESOLATION OF THE VILLAGE.

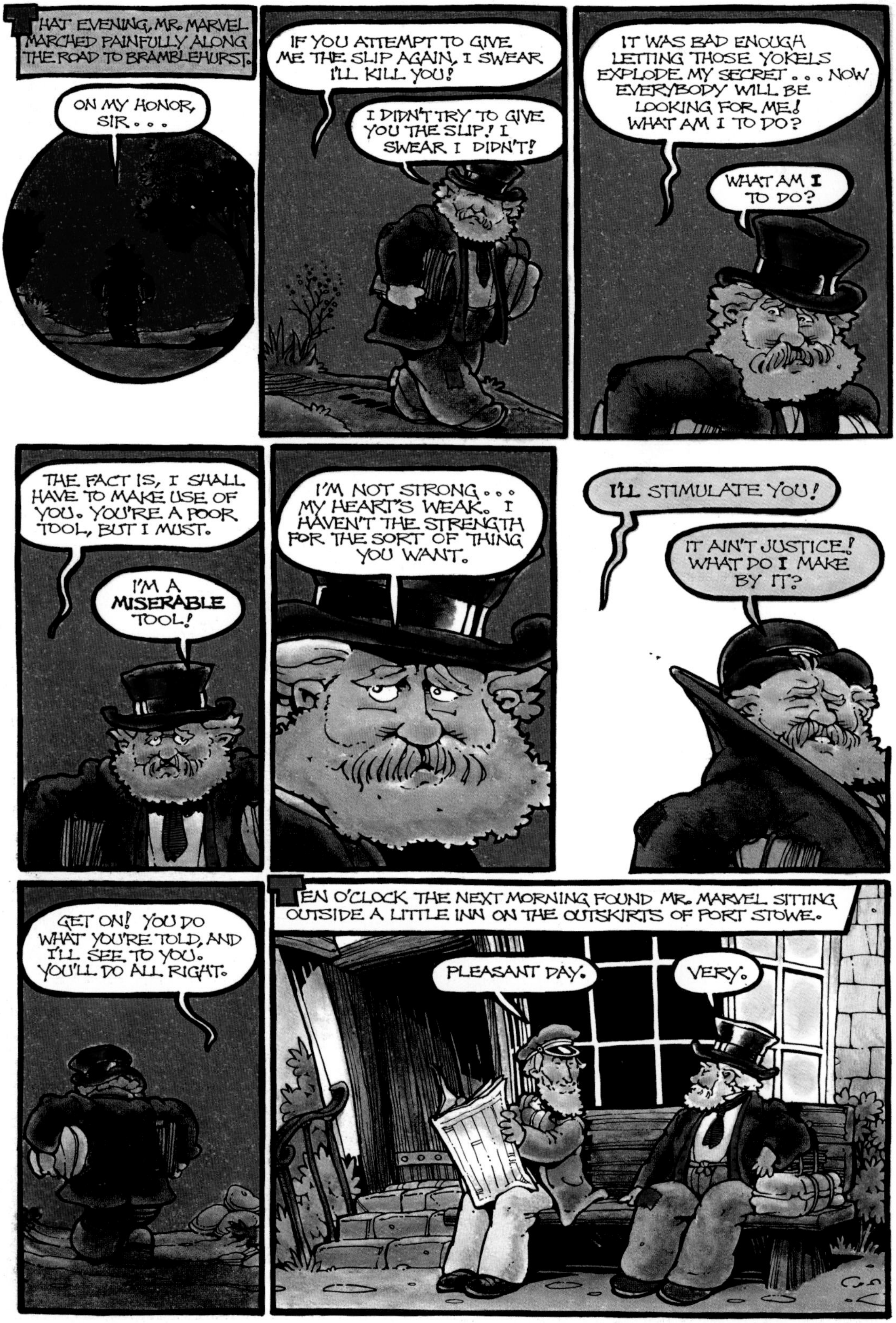
THAT EVENING, MR. MARVEL MARCHED PAINFULLY ALONG THE ROAD TO BRAMBLEHURST.
ON MY HONOR, SIR . . .
IF YOU ATTEMPT TO GIVE ME THE SLIP AGAIN, I SWEAR I'LL KILL YOU!
I DIDN'T TRY TO GIVE YOU THE SLIP! I SWEAR I DIDN'T!
IT WAS BAD ENOUGH LETTING THOSE YOKELS EXPLODE MY SECRET . . . NOW EVERYBODY WILL BE LOOKING FOR ME! WHAT AM I TO DO?
WHAT AM **I** TO DO?
THE FACT IS, I SHALL HAVE TO MAKE USE OF YOU. YOU'RE A POOR TOOL, BUT I MUST.
I'M A **MISERABLE** TOOL!
I'M NOT STRONG . . . MY HEART'S WEAK. I HAVEN'T THE STRENGTH FOR THE SORT OF THING YOU WANT.
I'LL STIMULATE YOU!
IT AIN'T JUSTICE! WHAT DO **I** MAKE BY IT?
GET ON! YOU DO WHAT YOU'RE TOLD, AND I'LL SEE TO YOU. YOU'LL DO ALL RIGHT.
TEN O'CLOCK THE NEXT MORNING FOUND MR. MARVEL SITTING OUTSIDE A LITTLE INN ON THE OUTSKIRTS OF PORT STOWE.
PLEASANT DAY.
VERY.

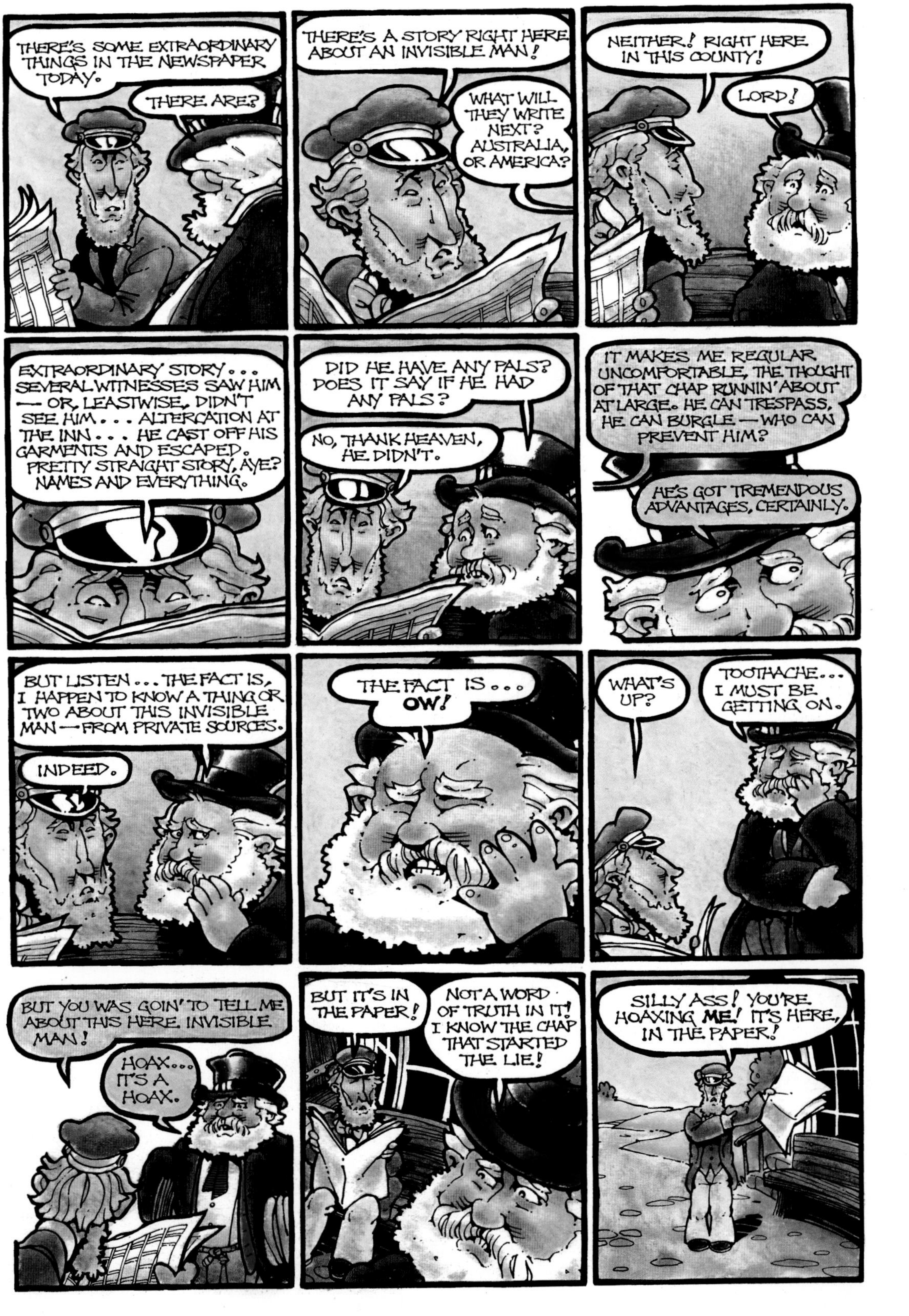
THERE'S SOME EXTRAORDINARY THINGS IN THE NEWSPAPER TODAY.
THERE ARE?
THERE'S A STORY RIGHT HERE ABOUT AN INVISIBLE MAN!
WHAT WILL THEY WRITE NEXT? AUSTRALIA, OR AMERICA?
NEITHER! RIGHT HERE IN THIS COUNTY!
LORD!
EXTRAORDINARY STORY... SEVERAL WITNESSES SAW HIM — OR, LEASTWISE, DIDN'T SEE HIM... ALTERCATION AT THE INN... HE CAST OFF HIS GARMENTS AND ESCAPED. PRETTY STRAIGHT STORY, AYE? NAMES AND EVERYTHING.
DID HE HAVE ANY PALS? DOES IT SAY IF HE HAD ANY PALS?
NO, THANK HEAVEN, HE DIDN'T.
IT MAKES ME REGULAR UNCOMFORTABLE, THE THOUGHT OF THAT CHAP RUNNIN' ABOUT AT LARGE. HE CAN TRESPASS, HE CAN BURGLE — WHO CAN PREVENT HIM?
HE'S GOT TREMENDOUS ADVANTAGES, CERTAINLY.
BUT LISTEN... THE FACT IS, I HAPPEN TO KNOW A THING OR TWO ABOUT THIS INVISIBLE MAN — FROM PRIVATE SOURCES.
INDEED.
THE FACT IS... OW!
WHAT'S UP?
TOOTHACHE... I MUST BE GETTING ON.
BUT YOU WAS GOIN' TO TELL ME ABOUT THIS HERE INVISIBLE MAN!
HOAX... IT'S A HOAX.
BUT IT'S IN THE PAPER!
NOT A WORD OF TRUTH IN IT! I KNOW THE CHAP THAT STARTED THE LIE!
SILLY ASS! YOU'RE HOAXING ME! IT'S HERE, IN THE PAPER!

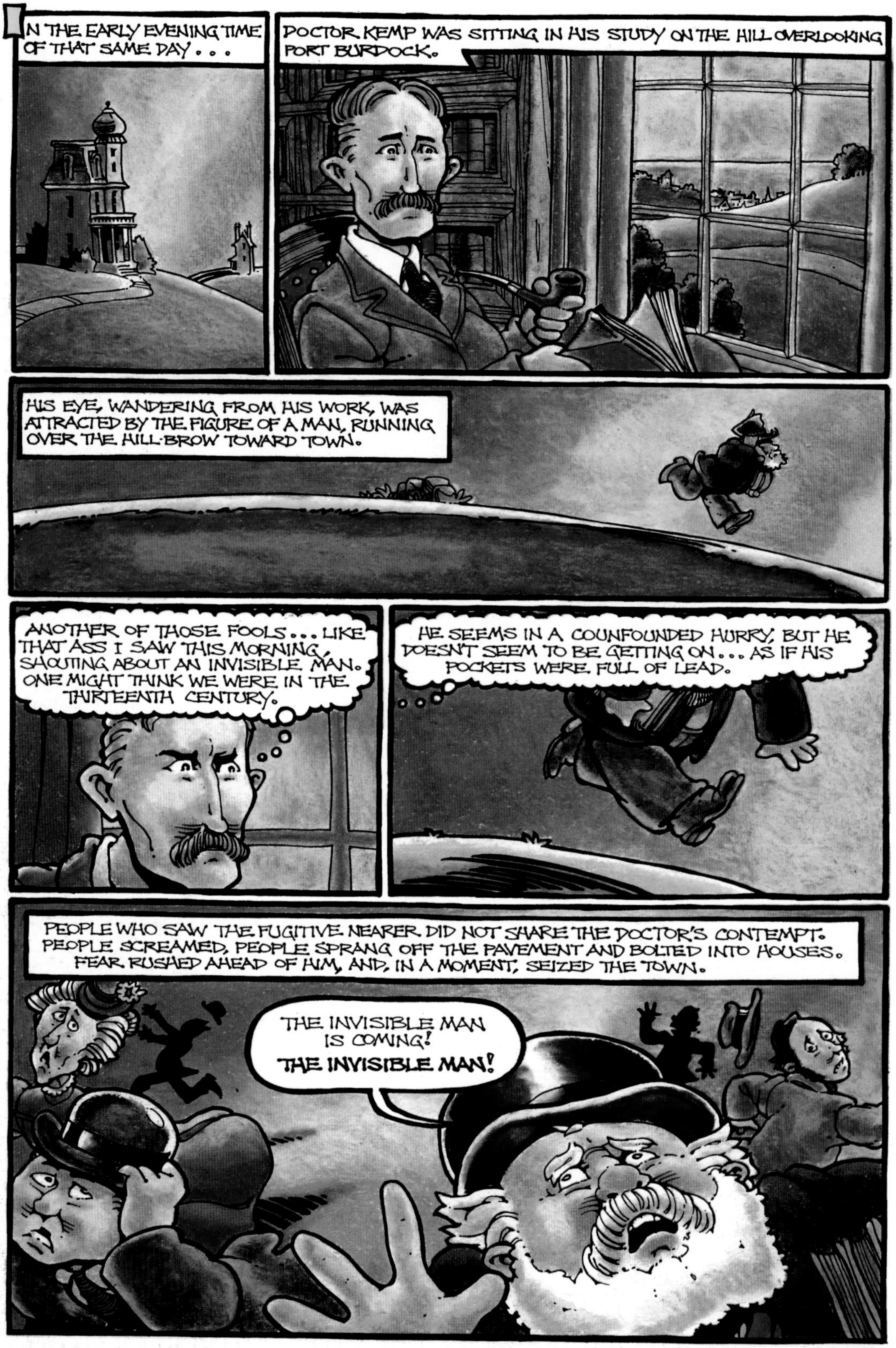
IN THE EARLY EVENING TIME OF THAT SAME DAY . . .
DOCTOR KEMP WAS SITTING IN HIS STUDY ON THE HILL OVERLOOKING PORT BURDOCK.
HIS EYE, WANDERING FROM HIS WORK, WAS ATTRACTED BY THE FIGURE OF A MAN, RUNNING OVER THE HILL-BROW TOWARD TOWN.
ANOTHER OF THOSE FOOLS . . . LIKE THAT ASS I SAW THIS MORNING, SHOUTING ABOUT AN INVISIBLE MAN. ONE MIGHT THINK WE WERE IN THE THIRTEENTH CENTURY.
HE SEEMS IN A COUNFOUNDED HURRY, BUT HE DOESN'T SEEM TO BE GETTING ON . . . AS IF HIS POCKETS WERE FULL OF LEAD.
PEOPLE WHO SAW THE FUGITIVE NEARER DID NOT SHARE THE DOCTOR'S CONTEMPT. PEOPLE SCREAMED, PEOPLE SPRANG OFF THE PAVEMENT AND BOLTED INTO HOUSES. FEAR RUSHED AHEAD OF HIM, AND, IN A MOMENT, SEIZED THE TOWN.
THE INVISIBLE MAN IS COMING! THE INVISIBLE MAN!

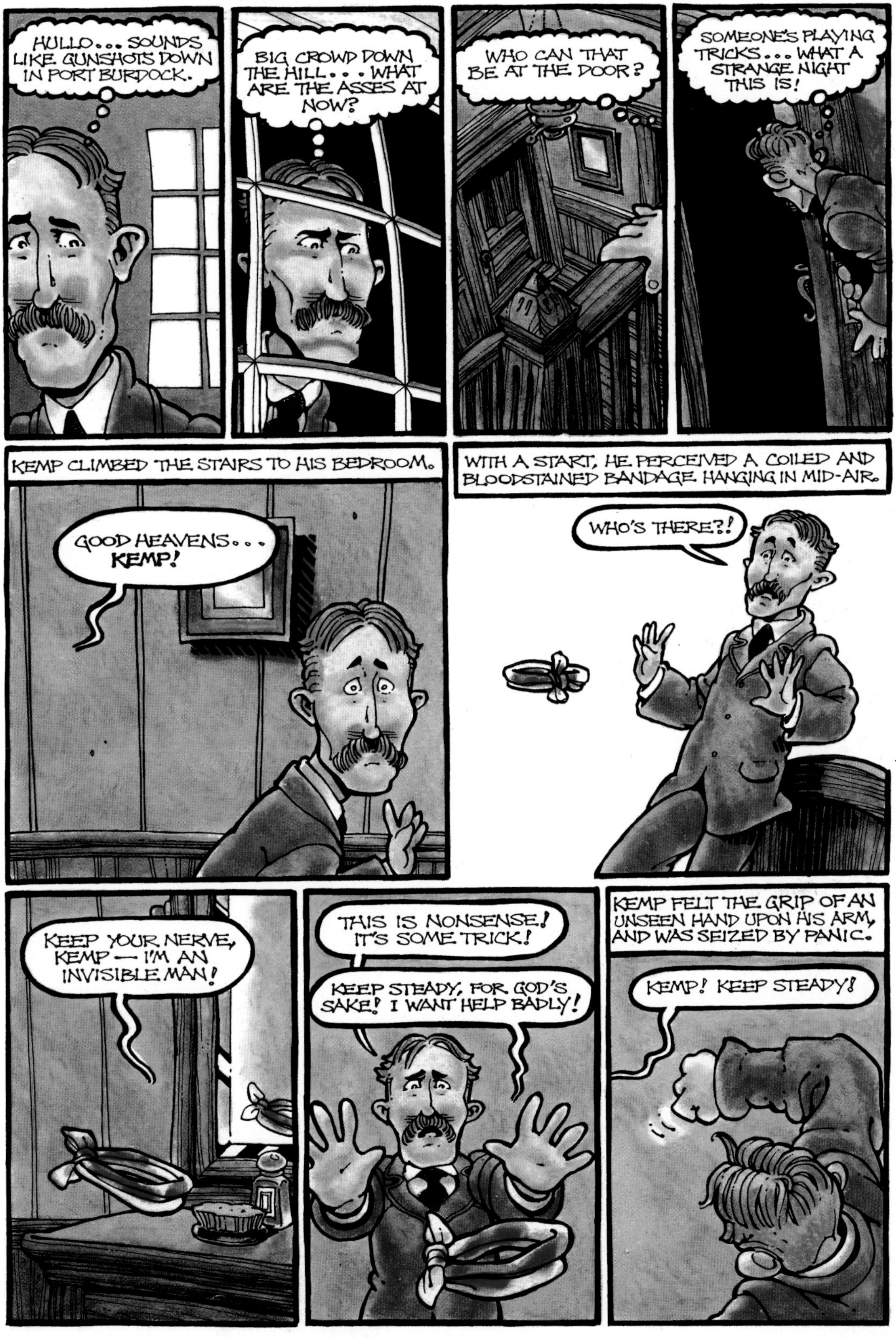
HULLO... SOUNDS LIKE GUNSHOTS DOWN IN PORT BURDOCK.
BIG CROWD DOWN THE HILL... WHAT ARE THE ASSES AT NOW?
WHO CAN THAT BE AT THE DOOR?
SOMEONE'S PLAYING TRICKS... WHAT A STRANGE NIGHT THIS IS!
KEMP CLIMBED THE STAIRS TO HIS BEDROOM.
GOOD HEAVENS... KEMP!
WITH A START, HE PERCEIVED A COILED AND BLOODSTAINED BANDAGE HANGING IN MID-AIR.
WHO'S THERE?!
KEEP YOUR NERVE, KEMP — I'M AN INVISIBLE MAN!
THIS IS NONSENSE! IT'S SOME TRICK!
KEEP STEADY, FOR GOD'S SAKE! I WANT HELP BADLY!
KEMP FELT THE GRIP OF AN UNSEEN HAND UPON HIS ARM, AND WAS SEIZED BY PANIC.
KEMP! KEEP STEADY!

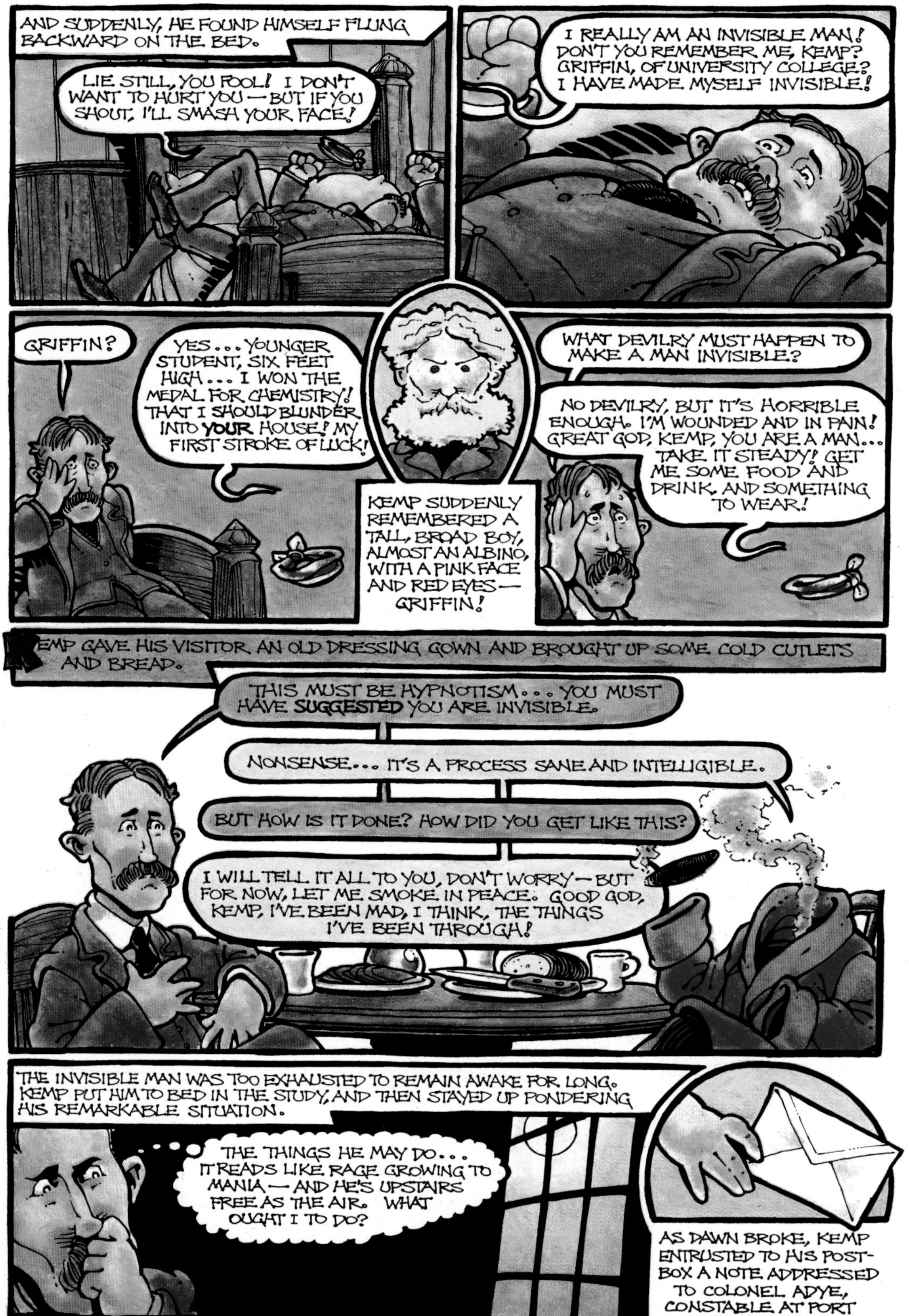
AND SUDDENLY, HE FOUND HIMSELF FLUNG BACKWARD ON THE BED.
LIE STILL, YOU FOOL! I DON'T WANT TO HURT YOU — BUT IF YOU SHOUT, I'LL SMASH YOUR FACE!
I REALLY AM AN INVISIBLE MAN! DON'T YOU REMEMBER ME, KEMP? GRIFFIN, OF UNIVERSITY COLLEGE? I HAVE MADE MYSELF INVISIBLE!
GRIFFIN?
YES... YOUNGER STUDENT, SIX FEET HIGH... I WON THE MEDAL FOR CHEMISTRY! THAT I SHOULD BLUNDER INTO YOUR HOUSE! MY FIRST STROKE OF LUCK!
KEMP SUDDENLY REMEMBERED A TALL, BROAD BOY, ALMOST AN ALBINO, WITH A PINK FACE AND RED EYES — GRIFFIN!
WHAT DEVILRY MUST HAPPEN TO MAKE A MAN INVISIBLE?
NO DEVILRY, BUT IT'S HORRIBLE ENOUGH. I'M WOUNDED AND IN PAIN! GREAT GOD, KEMP, YOU ARE A MAN... TAKE IT STEADY! GET ME SOME FOOD AND DRINK, AND SOMETHING TO WEAR!
KEMP GAVE HIS VISITOR AN OLD DRESSING GOWN AND BROUGHT UP SOME COLD CUTLETS AND BREAD.
THIS MUST BE HYPNOTISM... YOU MUST HAVE SUGGESTED YOU ARE INVISIBLE.
NONSENSE... IT'S A PROCESS SANE AND INTELLIGIBLE.
BUT HOW IS IT DONE? HOW DID YOU GET LIKE THIS?
I WILL TELL IT ALL TO YOU, DON'T WORRY — BUT FOR NOW, LET ME SMOKE IN PEACE. GOOD GOD, KEMP, I'VE BEEN MAD, I THINK, THE THINGS I'VE BEEN THROUGH!
THE INVISIBLE MAN WAS TOO EXHAUSTED TO REMAIN AWAKE FOR LONG. KEMP PUT HIM TO BED IN THE STUDY, AND THEN STAYED UP PONDERING HIS REMARKABLE SITUATION.
THE THINGS HE MAY DO... IT READS LIKE RAGE GROWING TO MANIA — AND HE'S UPSTAIRS FREE AS THE AIR. WHAT OUGHT I TO DO?
AS DAWN BROKE, KEMP ENTRUSTED TO HIS POST-BOX A NOTE ADDRESSED TO COLONEL ADYE, CONSTABLE AT PORT BURDOCK.

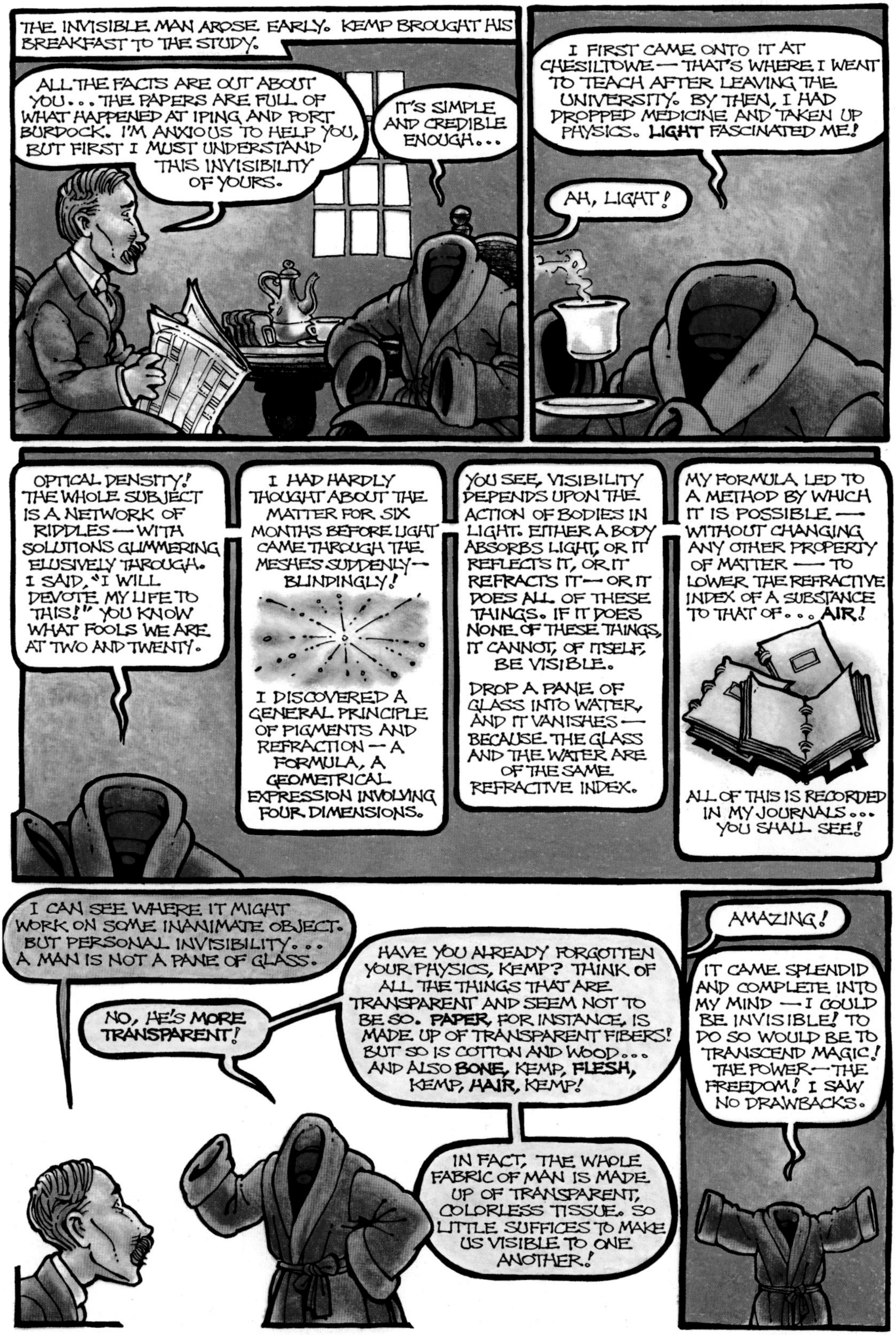
THE INVISIBLE MAN AROSE EARLY. KEMP BROUGHT HIS BREAKFAST TO THE STUDY.
ALL THE FACTS ARE OUT ABOUT YOU... THE PAPERS ARE FULL OF WHAT HAPPENED AT IPING AND PORT BURDOCK. I'M ANXIOUS TO HELP YOU, BUT FIRST I MUST UNDERSTAND THIS INVISIBILITY OF YOURS.
IT'S SIMPLE AND CREDIBLE ENOUGH...
I FIRST CAME ONTO IT AT CHESILTOWE — THAT'S WHERE I WENT TO TEACH AFTER LEAVING THE UNIVERSITY. BY THEN, I HAD DROPPED MEDICINE AND TAKEN UP PHYSICS. LIGHT FASCINATED ME!
AH, LIGHT!
OPTICAL DENSITY! THE WHOLE SUBJECT IS A NETWORK OF RIDDLES — WITH SOLUTIONS GLIMMERING ELUSIVELY THROUGH. I SAID, "I WILL DEVOTE MY LIFE TO THIS!" YOU KNOW WHAT FOOLS WE ARE AT TWO AND TWENTY.
I HAD HARDLY THOUGHT ABOUT THE MATTER FOR SIX MONTHS BEFORE LIGHT CAME THROUGH THE MESHES SUDDENLY — BLINDINGLY!
I DISCOVERED A GENERAL PRINCIPLE OF PIGMENTS AND REFRACTION — A FORMULA, A GEOMETRICAL EXPRESSION INVOLVING FOUR DIMENSIONS.
YOU SEE, VISIBILITY DEPENDS UPON THE ACTION OF BODIES IN LIGHT. EITHER A BODY ABSORBS LIGHT, OR IT REFLECTS IT, OR IT REFRACTS IT — OR IT DOES ALL OF THESE THINGS. IF IT DOES NONE OF THESE THINGS, IT CANNOT, OF ITSELF, BE VISIBLE.
DROP A PANE OF GLASS INTO WATER, AND IT VANISHES — BECAUSE THE GLASS AND THE WATER ARE OF THE SAME REFRACTIVE INDEX.
MY FORMULA LED TO A METHOD BY WHICH IT IS POSSIBLE — WITHOUT CHANGING ANY OTHER PROPERTY OF MATTER — TO LOWER THE REFRACTIVE INDEX OF A SUBSTANCE TO THAT OF... AIR!
ALL OF THIS IS RECORDED IN MY JOURNALS... YOU SHALL SEE!
I CAN SEE WHERE IT MIGHT WORK ON SOME INANIMATE OBJECT. BUT PERSONAL INVISIBILITY... A MAN IS NOT A PANE OF GLASS.
NO, HE'S MORE TRANSPARENT!
HAVE YOU ALREADY FORGOTTEN YOUR PHYSICS, KEMP? THINK OF ALL THE THINGS THAT ARE TRANSPARENT AND SEEM NOT TO BE SO. PAPER, FOR INSTANCE, IS MADE UP OF TRANSPARENT FIBERS! BUT SO IS COTTON AND WOOD... AND ALSO BONE, KEMP, FLESH, KEMP, HAIR, KEMP!
IN FACT, THE WHOLE FABRIC OF MAN IS MADE UP OF TRANSPARENT, COLORLESS TISSUE. SO LITTLE SUFFICES TO MAKE US VISIBLE TO ONE ANOTHER!
AMAZING!
IT CAME SPLENDID AND COMPLETE INTO MY MIND — I COULD BE INVISIBLE! TO DO SO WOULD BE TO TRANSCEND MAGIC! THE POWER — THE FREEDOM! I SAW NO DRAWBACKS.

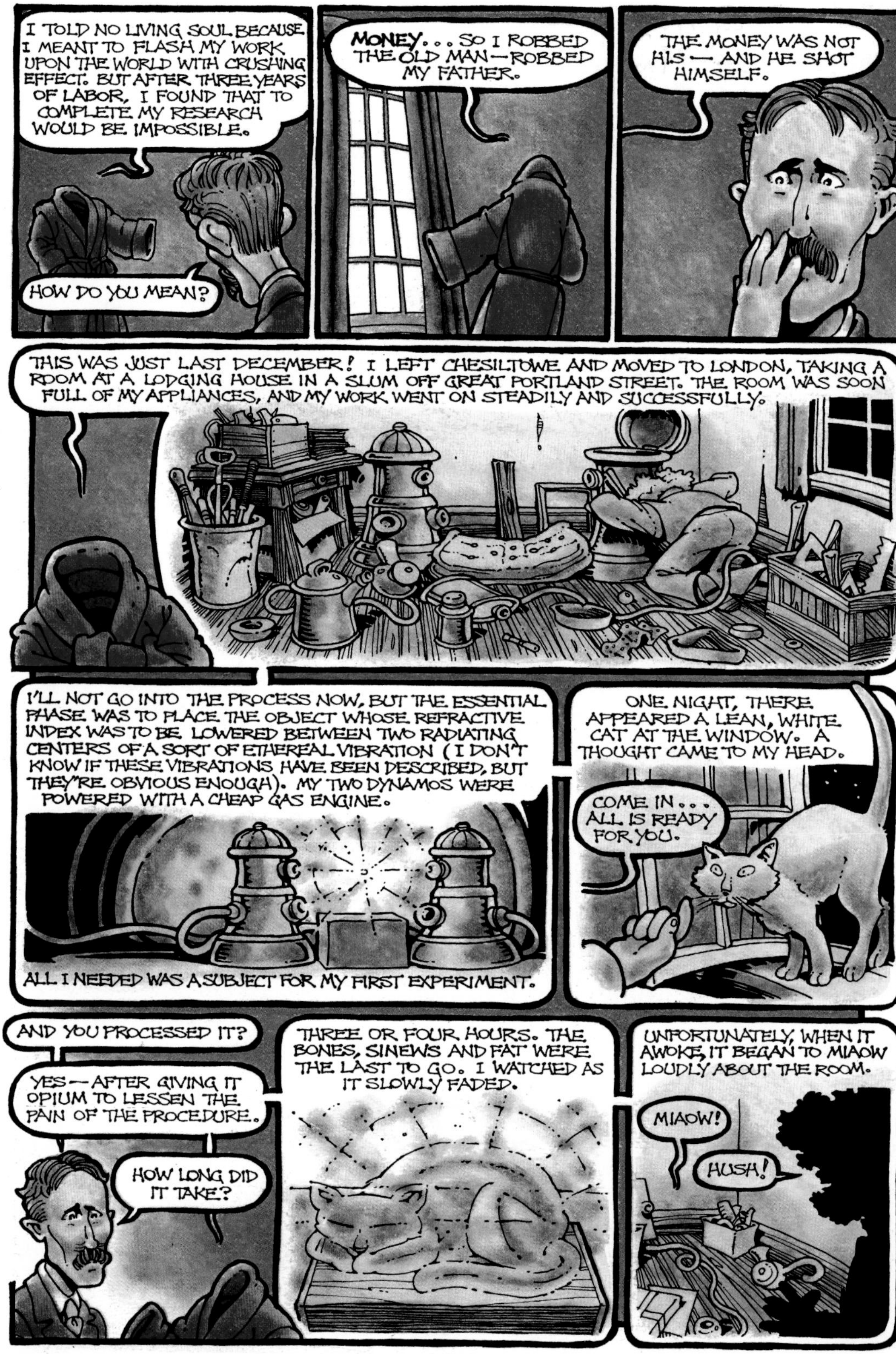
I TOLD NO LIVING SOUL BECAUSE I MEANT TO FLASH MY WORK UPON THE WORLD WITH CRUSHING EFFECT. BUT AFTER THREE YEARS OF LABOR, I FOUND THAT TO COMPLETE MY RESEARCH WOULD BE IMPOSSIBLE.
HOW DO YOU MEAN?
MONEY... SO I ROBBED THE OLD MAN — ROBBED MY FATHER.
THE MONEY WAS NOT HIS — AND HE SHOT HIMSELF.
THIS WAS JUST LAST DECEMBER! I LEFT CHESILTOWE AND MOVED TO LONDON, TAKING A ROOM AT A LODGING HOUSE IN A SLUM OFF GREAT PORTLAND STREET. THE ROOM WAS SOON FULL OF MY APPLIANCES, AND MY WORK WENT ON STEADILY AND SUCCESSFULLY.
I'LL NOT GO INTO THE PROCESS NOW, BUT THE ESSENTIAL PHASE WAS TO PLACE THE OBJECT WHOSE REFRACTIVE INDEX WAS TO BE LOWERED BETWEEN TWO RADIATING CENTERS OF A SORT OF ETHEREAL VIBRATION (I DON'T KNOW IF THESE VIBRATIONS HAVE BEEN DESCRIBED, BUT THEY'RE OBVIOUS ENOUGH). MY TWO DYNAMOS WERE POWERED WITH A CHEAP GAS ENGINE.
ALL I NEEDED WAS A SUBJECT FOR MY FIRST EXPERIMENT.
ONE NIGHT, THERE APPEARED A LEAN, WHITE CAT AT THE WINDOW. A THOUGHT CAME TO MY HEAD.
COME IN... ALL IS READY FOR YOU.
AND YOU PROCESSED IT?
YES — AFTER GIVING IT OPIUM TO LESSEN THE PAIN OF THE PROCEDURE.
HOW LONG DID IT TAKE?
THREE OR FOUR HOURS. THE BONES, SINEWS AND FAT WERE THE LAST TO GO. I WATCHED AS IT SLOWLY FADED.
UNFORTUNATELY, WHEN IT AWOKE, IT BEGAN TO MIAOW LOUDLY ABOUT THE ROOM.
MIAOW!
HUSH!

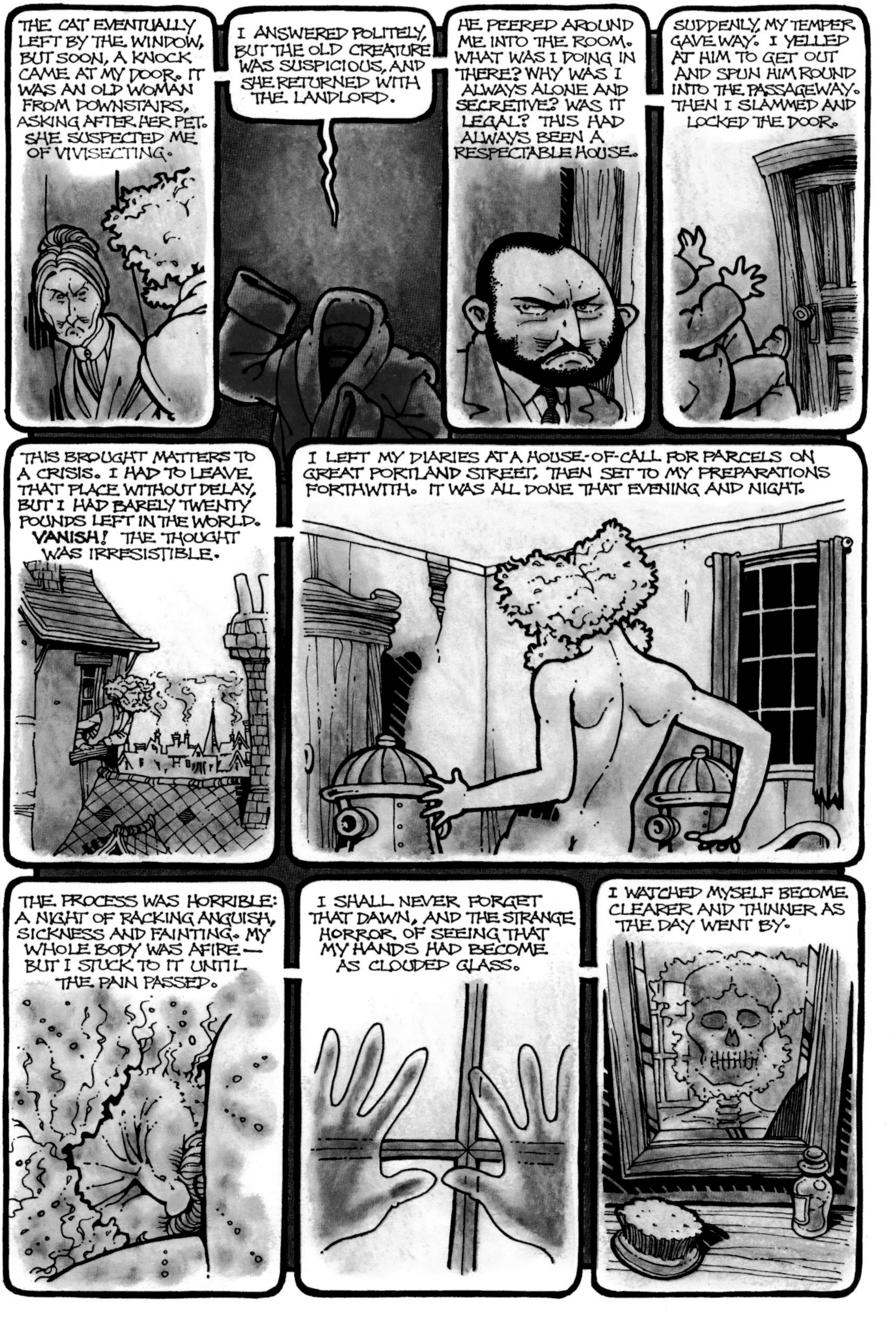

THE CAT EVENTUALLY LEFT BY THE WINDOW, BUT SOON, A KNOCK CAME AT MY DOOR. IT WAS AN OLD WOMAN FROM DOWNSTAIRS, ASKING AFTER HER PET. SHE SUSPECTED ME OF VIVISECTING.
I ANSWERED POLITELY, BUT THE OLD CREATURE WAS SUSPICIOUS, AND SHE RETURNED WITH THE LANDLORD.
HE PEERED AROUND ME INTO THE ROOM. WHAT WAS I DOING IN THERE? WHY WAS I ALWAYS ALONE AND SECRETIVE? WAS IT LEGAL? THIS HAD ALWAYS BEEN A RESPECTABLE HOUSE.
SUDDENLY, MY TEMPER GAVE WAY. I YELLED AT HIM TO GET OUT AND SPUN HIM ROUND INTO THE PASSAGEWAY. THEN I SLAMMED AND LOCKED THE DOOR.
THIS BROUGHT MATTERS TO A CRISIS. I HAD TO LEAVE THAT PLACE WITHOUT DELAY, BUT I HAD BARELY TWENTY POUNDS LEFT IN THE WORLD. VANISH! THE THOUGHT WAS IRRESISTIBLE.
I LEFT MY DIARIES AT A HOUSE-OF-CALL FOR PARCELS ON GREAT PORTLAND STREET, THEN SET TO MY PREPARATIONS FORTHWITH. IT WAS ALL DONE THAT EVENING AND NIGHT.
THE PROCESS WAS HORRIBLE: A NIGHT OF RACKING ANGUISH, SICKNESS AND FAINTING. MY WHOLE BODY WAS AFIRE — BUT I STUCK TO IT UNTIL THE PAIN PASSED.
I SHALL NEVER FORGET THAT DAWN, AND THE STRANGE HORROR OF SEEING THAT MY HANDS HAD BECOME AS CLOUDED GLASS.
I WATCHED MYSELF BECOME CLEARER AND THINNER AS THE DAY WENT BY.

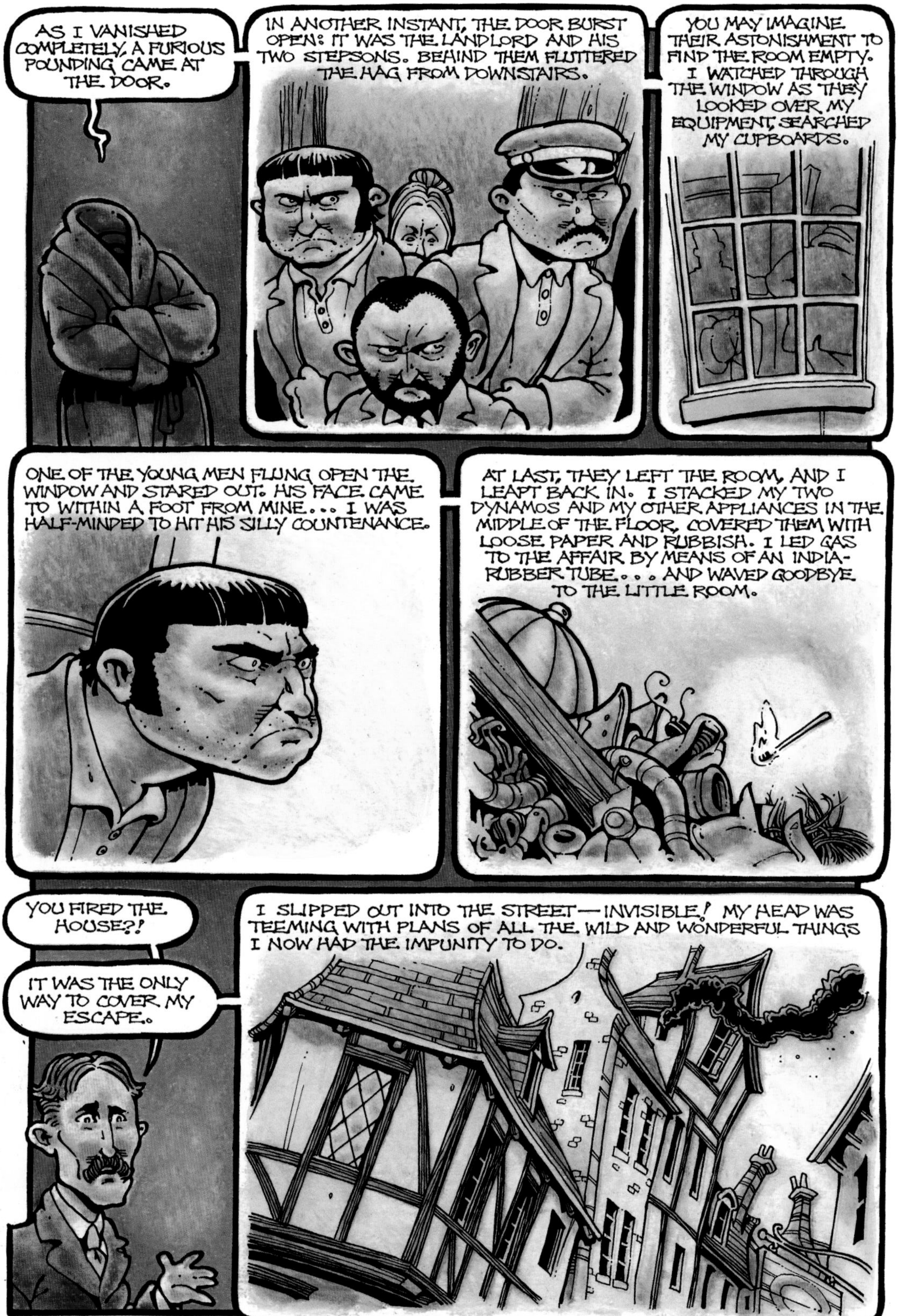
AS I VANISHED COMPLETELY, A FURIOUS POUNDING CAME AT THE DOOR.
IN ANOTHER INSTANT, THE DOOR BURST OPEN: IT WAS THE LANDLORD AND HIS TWO STEPSONS. BEHIND THEM FLUTTERED THE HAG FROM DOWNSTAIRS.
YOU MAY IMAGINE THEIR ASTONISHMENT TO FIND THE ROOM EMPTY. I WATCHED THROUGH THE WINDOW AS THEY LOOKED OVER MY EQUIPMENT, SEARCHED MY CUPBOARDS.
ONE OF THE YOUNG MEN FLUNG OPEN THE WINDOW AND STARED OUT. HIS FACE CAME TO WITHIN A FOOT FROM MINE... I WAS HALF-MINDED TO HIT HIS SILLY COUNTENANCE.
AT LAST, THEY LEFT THE ROOM, AND I LEAPT BACK IN. I STACKED MY TWO DYNAMOS AND MY OTHER APPLIANCES IN THE MIDDLE OF THE FLOOR, COVERED THEM WITH LOOSE PAPER AND RUBBISH. I LED GAS TO THE AFFAIR BY MEANS OF AN INDIA-RUBBER TUBE... AND WAVED GOODBYE TO THE LITTLE ROOM.
YOU FIRED THE HOUSE?!
IT WAS THE ONLY WAY TO COVER MY ESCAPE.
I SLIPPED OUT INTO THE STREET—INVISIBLE! MY HEAD WAS TEEMING WITH PLANS OF ALL THE WILD AND WONDERFUL THINGS I NOW HAD THE IMPUNITY TO DO.

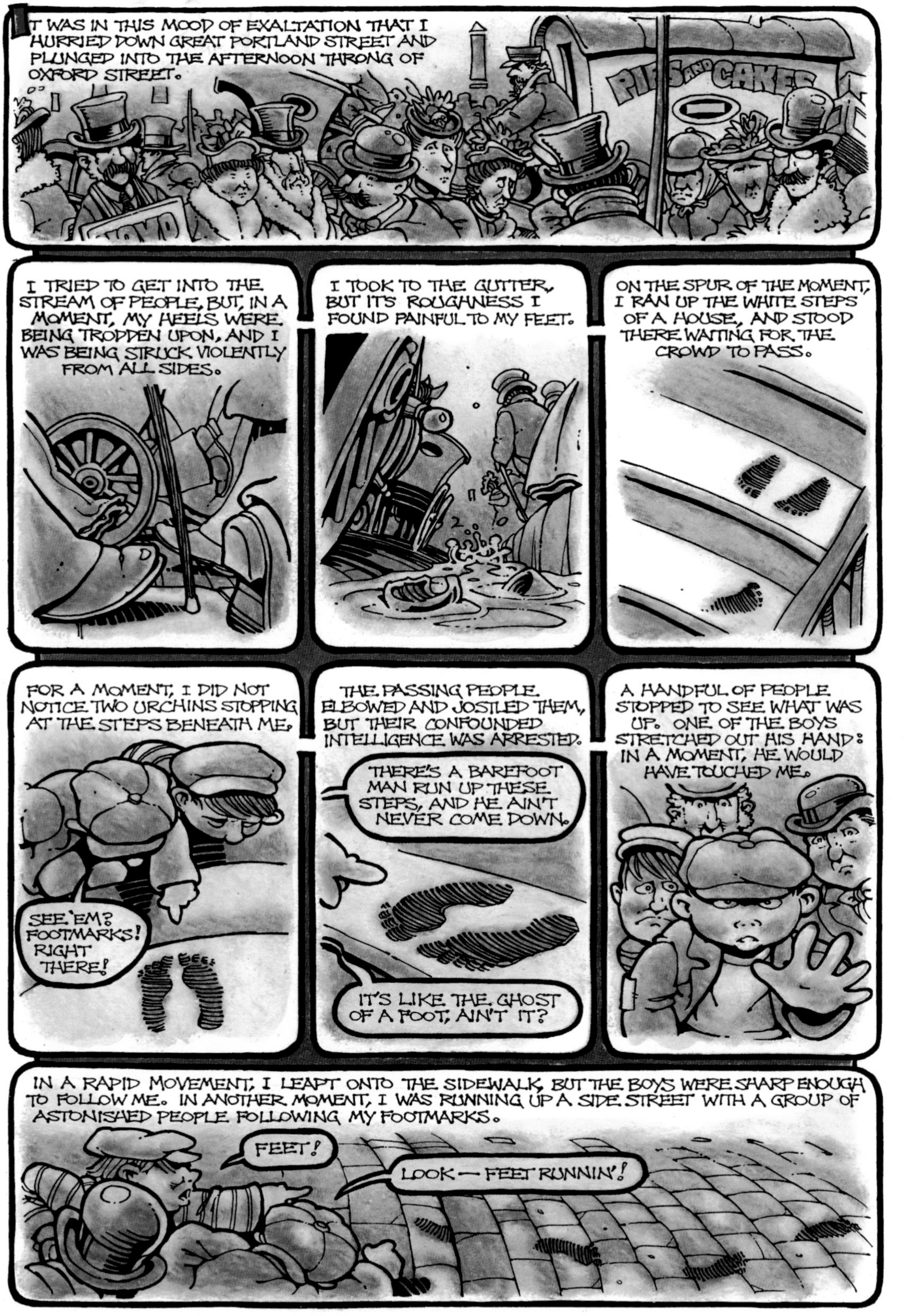
IT WAS IN THIS MOOD OF EXALTATION THAT I HURRIED DOWN GREAT PORTLAND STREET AND PLUNGED INTO THE AFTERNOON THRONG OF OXFORD STREET.
PIES AND CAKES
I TRIED TO GET INTO THE STREAM OF PEOPLE, BUT, IN A MOMENT, MY HEELS WERE BEING TRODDEN UPON, AND I WAS BEING STRUCK VIOLENTLY FROM ALL SIDES.
I TOOK TO THE GUTTER, BUT ITS ROUGHNESS I FOUND PAINFUL TO MY FEET.
ON THE SPUR OF THE MOMENT, I RAN UP THE WHITE STEPS OF A HOUSE, AND STOOD THERE WAITING FOR THE CROWD TO PASS.
FOR A MOMENT, I DID NOT NOTICE TWO URCHINS STOPPING AT THE STEPS BENEATH ME.
SEE 'EM? FOOTMARKS! RIGHT THERE!
THE PASSING PEOPLE ELBOWED AND JOSTLED THEM, BUT THEIR CONFOUNDED INTELLIGENCE WAS ARRESTED.
THERE'S A BAREFOOT MAN RUN UP THESE STEPS, AND HE AIN'T NEVER COME DOWN.
IT'S LIKE THE GHOST OF A FOOT, AIN'T IT?
A HANDFUL OF PEOPLE STOPPED TO SEE WHAT WAS UP. ONE OF THE BOYS STRETCHED OUT HIS HAND: IN A MOMENT, HE WOULD HAVE TOUCHED ME.
IN A RAPID MOVEMENT, I LEAPT ONTO THE SIDEWALK, BUT THE BOYS WERE SHARP ENOUGH TO FOLLOW ME. IN ANOTHER MOMENT, I WAS RUNNING UP A SIDE STREET WITH A GROUP OF ASTONISHED PEOPLE FOLLOWING MY FOOTMARKS.
FEET!
LOOK — FEET RUNNIN'!

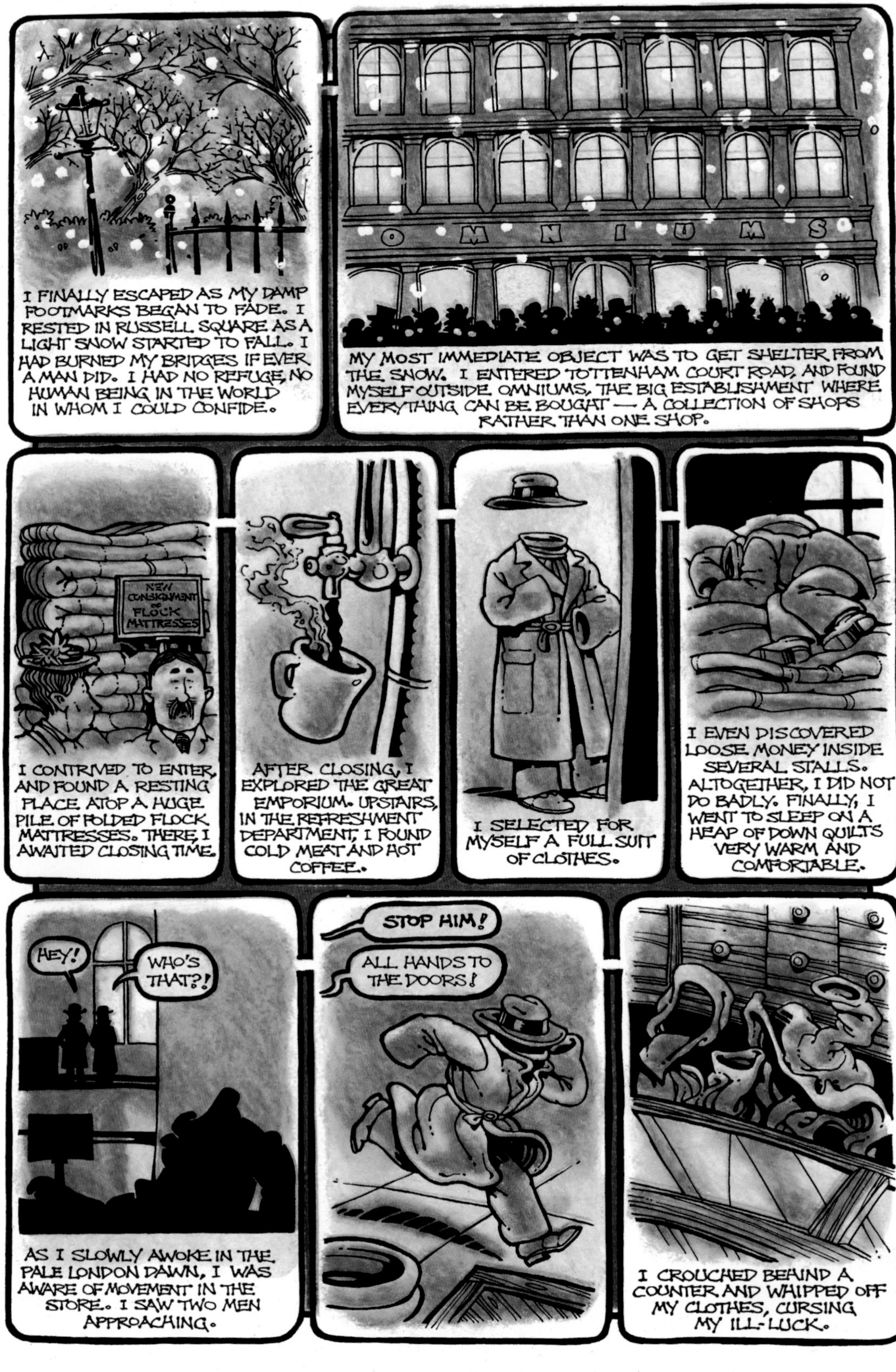

I FINALLY ESCAPED AS MY DAMP FOOTMARKS BEGAN TO FADE. I RESTED IN RUSSELL SQUARE AS A LIGHT SNOW STARTED TO FALL. I HAD BURNED MY BRIDGES IF EVER A MAN DID. I HAD NO REFUGE, NO HUMAN BEING IN THE WORLD IN WHOM I COULD CONFIDE.
OMNIUMS
MY MOST IMMEDIATE OBJECT WAS TO GET SHELTER FROM THE SNOW. I ENTERED TOTTENHAM COURT ROAD, AND FOUND MYSELF OUTSIDE OMNIUMS, THE BIG ESTABLISHMENT WHERE EVERYTHING CAN BE BOUGHT — A COLLECTION OF SHOPS RATHER THAN ONE SHOP.
NEW CONSIGNMENT OF FLOCK MATTRESSES
I CONTRIVED TO ENTER, AND FOUND A RESTING PLACE ATOP A HUGE PILE OF FOLDED FLOCK MATTRESSES. THERE I AWAITED CLOSING TIME.
AFTER CLOSING, I EXPLORED THE GREAT EMPORIUM. UPSTAIRS, IN THE REFRESHMENT DEPARTMENT, I FOUND COLD MEAT AND HOT COFFEE.
I SELECTED FOR MYSELF A FULL SUIT OF CLOTHES.
I EVEN DISCOVERED LOOSE MONEY INSIDE SEVERAL STALLS. ALTOGETHER, I DID NOT DO BADLY. FINALLY, I WENT TO SLEEP ON A HEAP OF DOWN QUILTS VERY WARM AND COMFORTABLE.
HEY!
WHO'S THAT?!
AS I SLOWLY AWOKE IN THE PALE LONDON DAWN, I WAS AWARE OF MOVEMENT IN THE STORE. I SAW TWO MEN APPROACHING.
STOP HIM!
ALL HANDS TO THE DOORS!
I CROUCHED BEHIND A COUNTER AND WHIPPED OFF MY CLOTHES, CURSING MY ILL-LUCK.

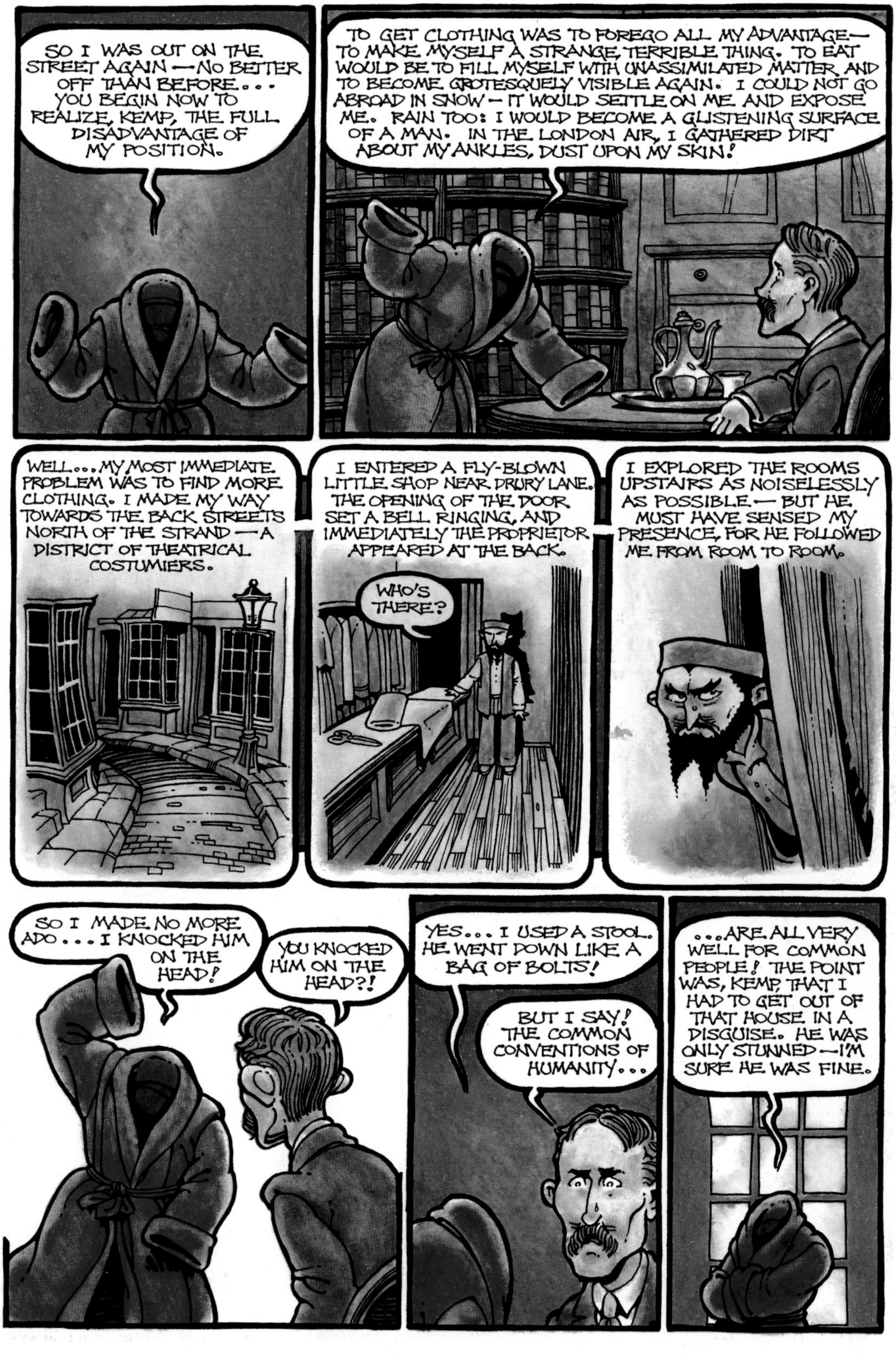
SO I WAS OUT ON THE STREET AGAIN — NO BETTER OFF THAN BEFORE... YOU BEGIN NOW TO REALIZE, KEMP, THE FULL DISADVANTAGE OF MY POSITION.
TO GET CLOTHING WAS TO FOREGO ALL MY ADVANTAGE— TO MAKE MYSELF A STRANGE, TERRIBLE THING. TO EAT WOULD BE TO FILL MYSELF WITH UNASSIMILATED MATTER AND TO BECOME GROTESQUELY VISIBLE AGAIN. I COULD NOT GO ABROAD IN SNOW — IT WOULD SETTLE ON ME AND EXPOSE ME. RAIN TOO: I WOULD BECOME A GLISTENING SURFACE OF A MAN. IN THE LONDON AIR, I GATHERED DIRT ABOUT MY ANKLES, DUST UPON MY SKIN!
WELL... MY MOST IMMEDIATE PROBLEM WAS TO FIND MORE CLOTHING. I MADE MY WAY TOWARDS THE BACK STREETS NORTH OF THE STRAND — A DISTRICT OF THEATRICAL COSTUMIERS.
I ENTERED A FLY-BLOWN LITTLE SHOP NEAR DRURY LANE. THE OPENING OF THE DOOR SET A BELL RINGING, AND IMMEDIATELY THE PROPRIETOR APPEARED AT THE BACK.
WHO'S THERE?
I EXPLORED THE ROOMS UPSTAIRS AS NOISELESSLY AS POSSIBLE — BUT HE MUST HAVE SENSED MY PRESENCE, FOR HE FOLLOWED ME FROM ROOM TO ROOM.
SO I MADE NO MORE ADO... I KNOCKED HIM ON THE HEAD!
YOU KNOCKED HIM ON THE HEAD?!
YES... I USED A STOOL. HE WENT DOWN LIKE A BAG OF BOLTS!
BUT I SAY! THE COMMON CONVENTIONS OF HUMANITY...
...ARE ALL VERY WELL FOR COMMON PEOPLE! THE POINT WAS, KEMP, THAT I HAD TO GET OUT OF THAT HOUSE IN A DISGUISE. HE WAS ONLY STUNNED — I'M SURE HE WAS FINE.

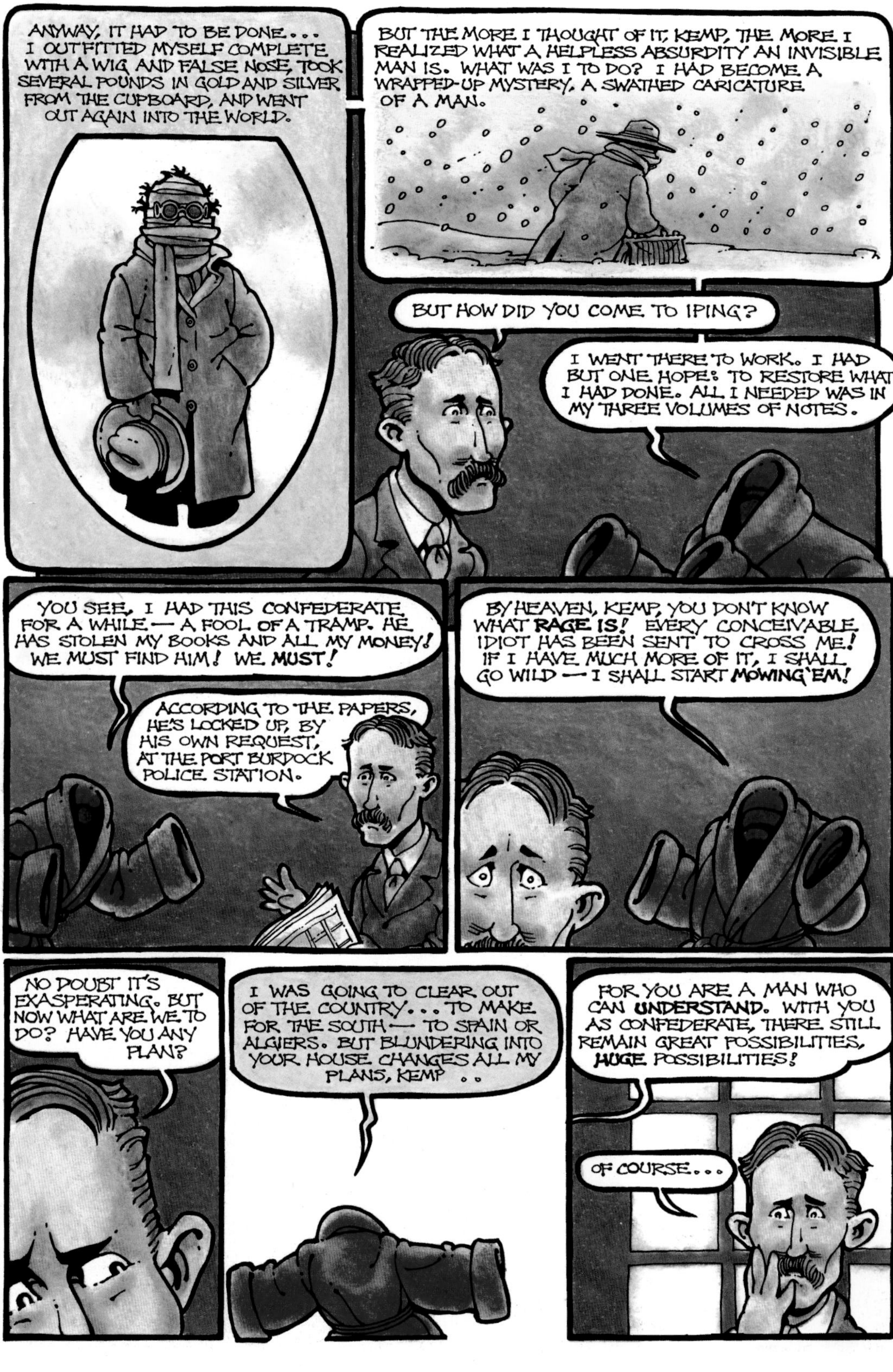

ANYWAY, IT HAD TO BE DONE... I OUTFITTED MYSELF COMPLETE WITH A WIG AND FALSE NOSE, TOOK SEVERAL POUNDS IN GOLD AND SILVER FROM THE CUPBOARD, AND WENT OUT AGAIN INTO THE WORLD.
BUT THE MORE I THOUGHT OF IT, KEMP, THE MORE I REALIZED WHAT A HELPLESS ABSURDITY AN INVISIBLE MAN IS. WHAT WAS I TO DO? I HAD BECOME A WRAPPED-UP MYSTERY, A SWATHED CARICATURE OF A MAN.
BUT HOW DID YOU COME TO IPING?
I WENT THERE TO WORK. I HAD BUT ONE HOPE: TO RESTORE WHAT I HAD DONE. ALL I NEEDED WAS IN MY THREE VOLUMES OF NOTES.
YOU SEE, I HAD THIS CONFEDERATE FOR A WHILE — A FOOL OF A TRAMP. HE HAS STOLEN MY BOOKS AND ALL MY MONEY! WE MUST FIND HIM! WE **MUST**!
ACCORDING TO THE PAPERS, HE'S LOCKED UP, BY HIS OWN REQUEST, AT THE PORT BURDOCK POLICE STATION.
BY HEAVEN, KEMP, YOU DON'T KNOW WHAT **RAGE IS**! EVERY CONCEIVABLE IDIOT HAS BEEN SENT TO CROSS ME! IF I HAVE MUCH MORE OF IT, I SHALL GO WILD — I SHALL START **MOWING 'EM**!
NO DOUBT IT'S EXASPERATING. BUT NOW WHAT ARE WE TO DO? HAVE YOU ANY PLAN?
I WAS GOING TO CLEAR OUT OF THE COUNTRY... TO MAKE FOR THE SOUTH — TO SPAIN OR ALGIERS. BUT BLUNDERING INTO YOUR HOUSE CHANGES ALL MY PLANS, KEMP..
FOR YOU ARE A MAN WHO CAN **UNDERSTAND**. WITH YOU AS CONFEDERATE, THERE STILL REMAIN GREAT POSSIBILITIES, **HUGE** POSSIBILITIES!
OF COURSE...

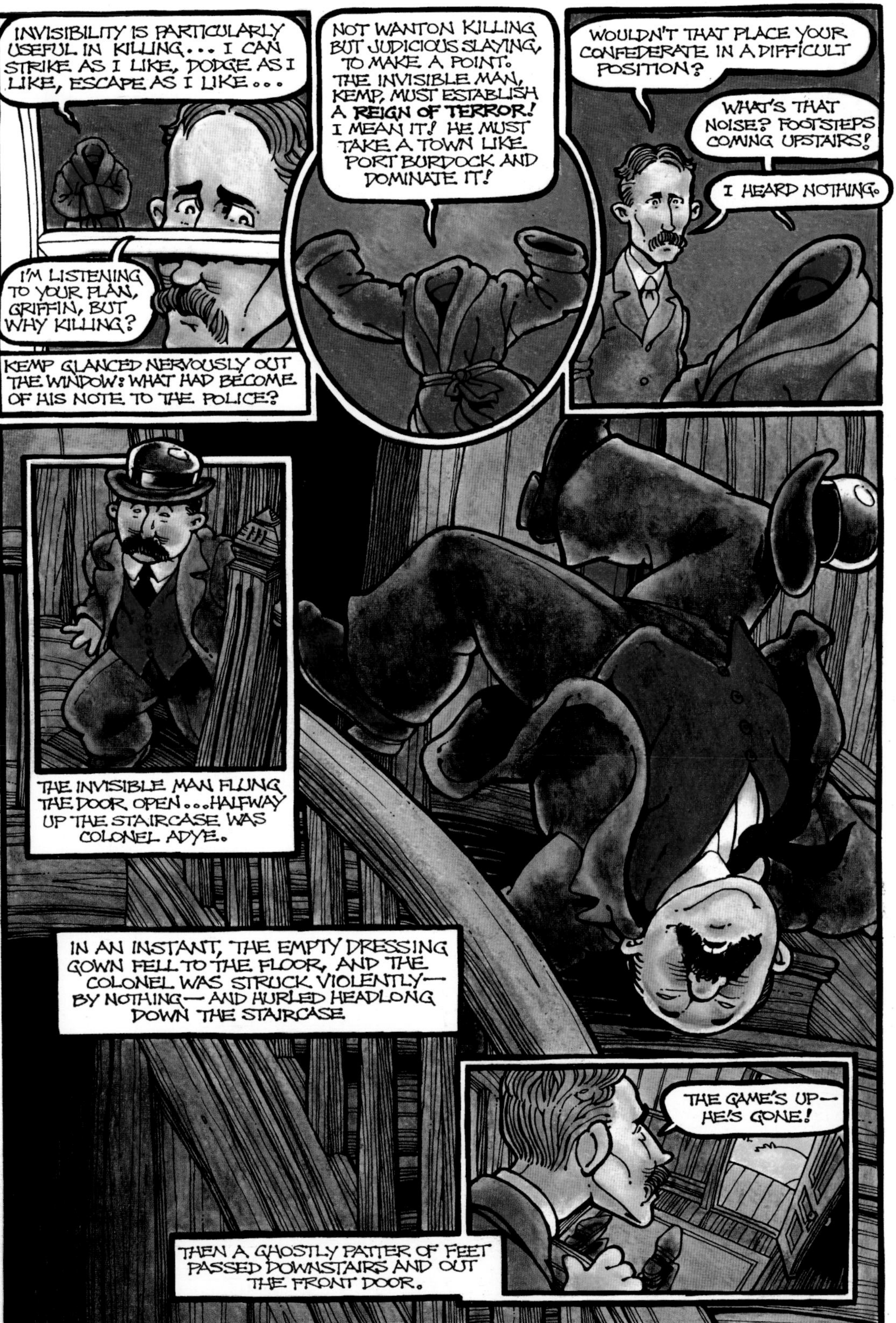

INVISIBILITY IS PARTICULARLY USEFUL IN KILLING... I CAN STRIKE AS I LIKE, DODGE AS I LIKE, ESCAPE AS I LIKE...
I'M LISTENING TO YOUR PLAN, GRIFFIN, BUT WHY KILLING?
KEMP GLANCED NERVOUSLY OUT THE WINDOW: WHAT HAD BECOME OF HIS NOTE TO THE POLICE?
NOT WANTON KILLING BUT JUDICIOUS SLAYING, TO MAKE A POINT. THE INVISIBLE MAN, KEMP, MUST ESTABLISH A REIGN OF TERROR! I MEAN IT! HE MUST TAKE A TOWN LIKE PORT BURDOCK AND DOMINATE IT!
WOULDN'T THAT PLACE YOUR CONFEDERATE IN A DIFFICULT POSITION?
WHAT'S THAT NOISE? FOOTSTEPS COMING UPSTAIRS!
I HEARD NOTHING.
THE INVISIBLE MAN FLUNG THE DOOR OPEN...HALFWAY UP THE STAIRCASE WAS COLONEL ADYE.
IN AN INSTANT, THE EMPTY DRESSING GOWN FELL TO THE FLOOR, AND THE COLONEL WAS STRUCK VIOLENTLY— BY NOTHING— AND HURLED HEADLONG DOWN THE STAIRCASE
THE GAME'S UP— HE'S GONE!
THEN A GHOSTLY PATTER OF FEET PASSED DOWNSTAIRS AND OUT THE FRONT DOOR.

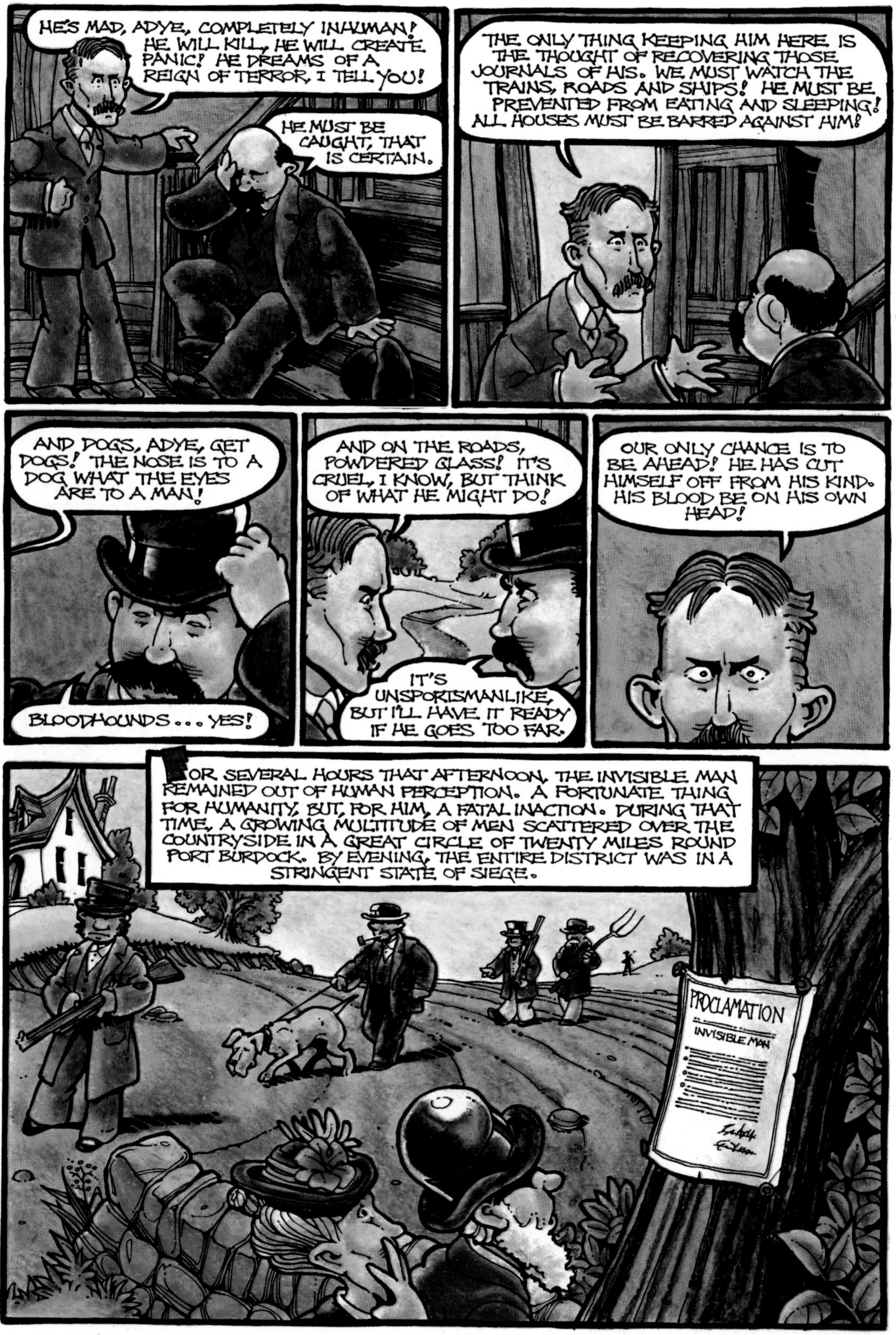
HE'S MAD, ADYE, COMPLETELY INHUMAN! HE WILL KILL, HE WILL CREATE PANIC! HE DREAMS OF A REIGN OF TERROR, I TELL YOU!
HE MUST BE CAUGHT, THAT IS CERTAIN.
THE ONLY THING KEEPING HIM HERE IS THE THOUGHT OF RECOVERING THOSE JOURNALS OF HIS. WE MUST WATCH THE TRAINS, ROADS AND SHIPS! HE MUST BE PREVENTED FROM EATING AND SLEEPING! ALL HOUSES MUST BE BARRED AGAINST HIM!
AND DOGS, ADYE, GET DOGS! THE NOSE IS TO A DOG WHAT THE EYES ARE TO A MAN!
BLOODHOUNDS . . . YES!
AND ON THE ROADS, POWDERED GLASS! IT'S CRUEL, I KNOW, BUT THINK OF WHAT HE MIGHT DO!
IT'S UNSPORTSMANLIKE, BUT I'LL HAVE IT READY IF HE GOES TOO FAR.
OUR ONLY CHANCE IS TO BE AHEAD! HE HAS CUT HIMSELF OFF FROM HIS KIND. HIS BLOOD BE ON HIS OWN HEAD!
FOR SEVERAL HOURS THAT AFTERNOON, THE INVISIBLE MAN REMAINED OUT OF HUMAN PERCEPTION. A FORTUNATE THING FOR HUMANITY, BUT, FOR HIM, A FATAL INACTION. DURING THAT TIME, A GROWING MULTITUDE OF MEN SCATTERED OVER THE COUNTRYSIDE IN A GREAT CIRCLE OF TWENTY MILES ROUND PORT BURDOCK. BY EVENING, THE ENTIRE DISTRICT WAS IN A STRINGENT STATE OF SIEGE.
PROCLAMATION
INVISIBLE MAN

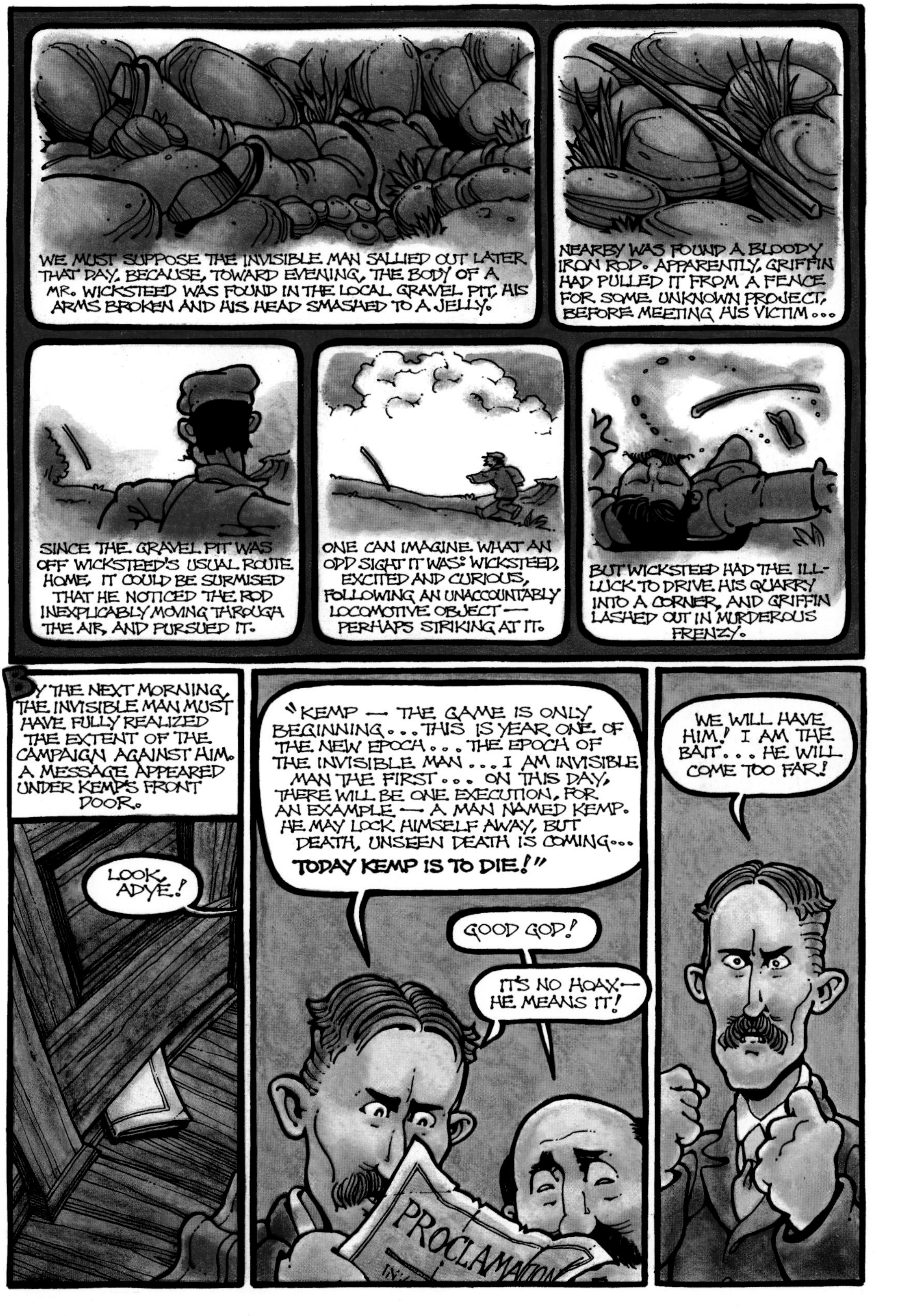
WE MUST SUPPOSE THE INVISIBLE MAN SALLIED OUT LATER THAT DAY, BECAUSE, TOWARD EVENING, THE BODY OF A MR. WICKSTEED WAS FOUND IN THE LOCAL GRAVEL PIT, HIS ARMS BROKEN AND HIS HEAD SMASHED TO A JELLY.
NEARBY WAS FOUND A BLOODY IRON ROD. APPARENTLY, GRIFFIN HAD PULLED IT FROM A FENCE FOR SOME UNKNOWN PROJECT, BEFORE MEETING HIS VICTIM...
SINCE THE GRAVEL PIT WAS OFF WICKSTEED'S USUAL ROUTE HOME, IT COULD BE SURMISED THAT HE NOTICED THE ROD INEXPLICABLY MOVING THROUGH THE AIR, AND PURSUED IT.
ONE CAN IMAGINE WHAT AN ODD SIGHT IT WAS: WICKSTEED, EXCITED AND CURIOUS, FOLLOWING AN UNACCOUNTABLY LOCOMOTIVE OBJECT — PERHAPS STRIKING AT IT.
BUT WICKSTEED HAD THE ILL-LUCK TO DRIVE HIS QUARRY INTO A CORNER, AND GRIFFIN LASHED OUT IN MURDEROUS FRENZY.
BY THE NEXT MORNING, THE INVISIBLE MAN MUST HAVE FULLY REALIZED THE EXTENT OF THE CAMPAIGN AGAINST HIM. A MESSAGE APPEARED UNDER KEMP'S FRONT DOOR.
LOOK, ADYE!
"KEMP — THE GAME IS ONLY BEGINNING... THIS IS YEAR ONE OF THE NEW EPOCH... THE EPOCH OF THE INVISIBLE MAN... I AM INVISIBLE MAN THE FIRST... ON THIS DAY, THERE WILL BE ONE EXECUTION, FOR AN EXAMPLE — A MAN NAMED KEMP. HE MAY LOCK HIMSELF AWAY, BUT DEATH, UNSEEN DEATH IS COMING... TODAY KEMP IS TO DIE!"
GOOD GOD!
IT'S NO HOAX — HE MEANS IT!
PROCLAMATION
WE WILL HAVE HIM! I AM THE BAIT... HE WILL COME TOO FAR!

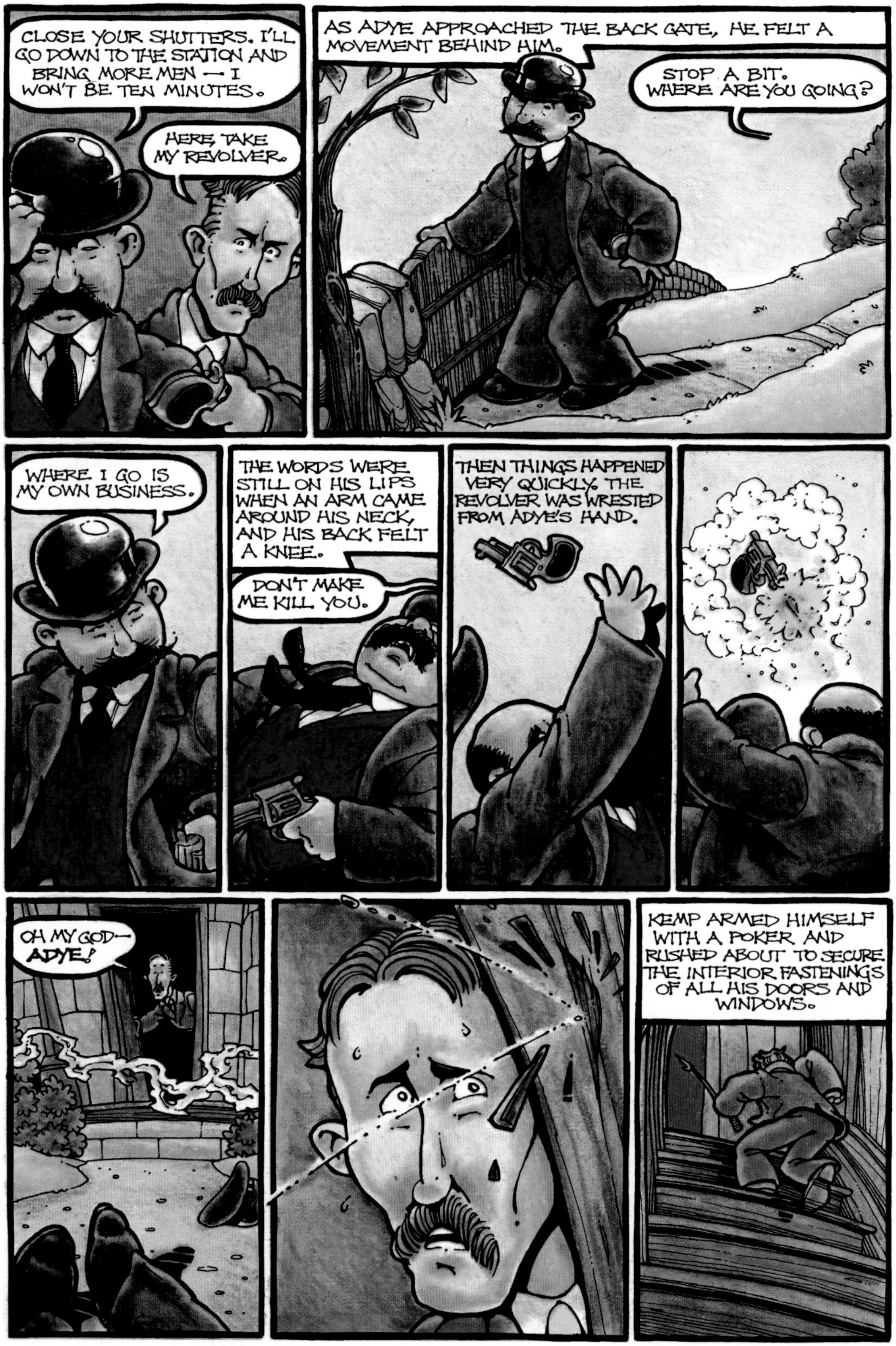

CLOSE YOUR SHUTTERS. I'LL GO DOWN TO THE STATION AND BRING MORE MEN — I WON'T BE TEN MINUTES.
HERE, TAKE MY REVOLVER.
AS ADYE APPROACHED THE BACK GATE, HE FELT A MOVEMENT BEHIND HIM.
STOP A BIT. WHERE ARE YOU GOING?
WHERE I GO IS MY OWN BUSINESS.
THE WORDS WERE STILL ON HIS LIPS WHEN AN ARM CAME AROUND HIS NECK, AND HIS BACK FELT A KNEE.
DON'T MAKE ME KILL YOU.
THEN THINGS HAPPENED VERY QUICKLY. THE REVOLVER WAS WRESTED FROM ADYE'S HAND.
OH MY GOD— ADYE!
KEMP ARMED HIMSELF WITH A POKER AND RUSHED ABOUT TO SECURE THE INTERIOR FASTENINGS OF ALL HIS DOORS AND WINDOWS.

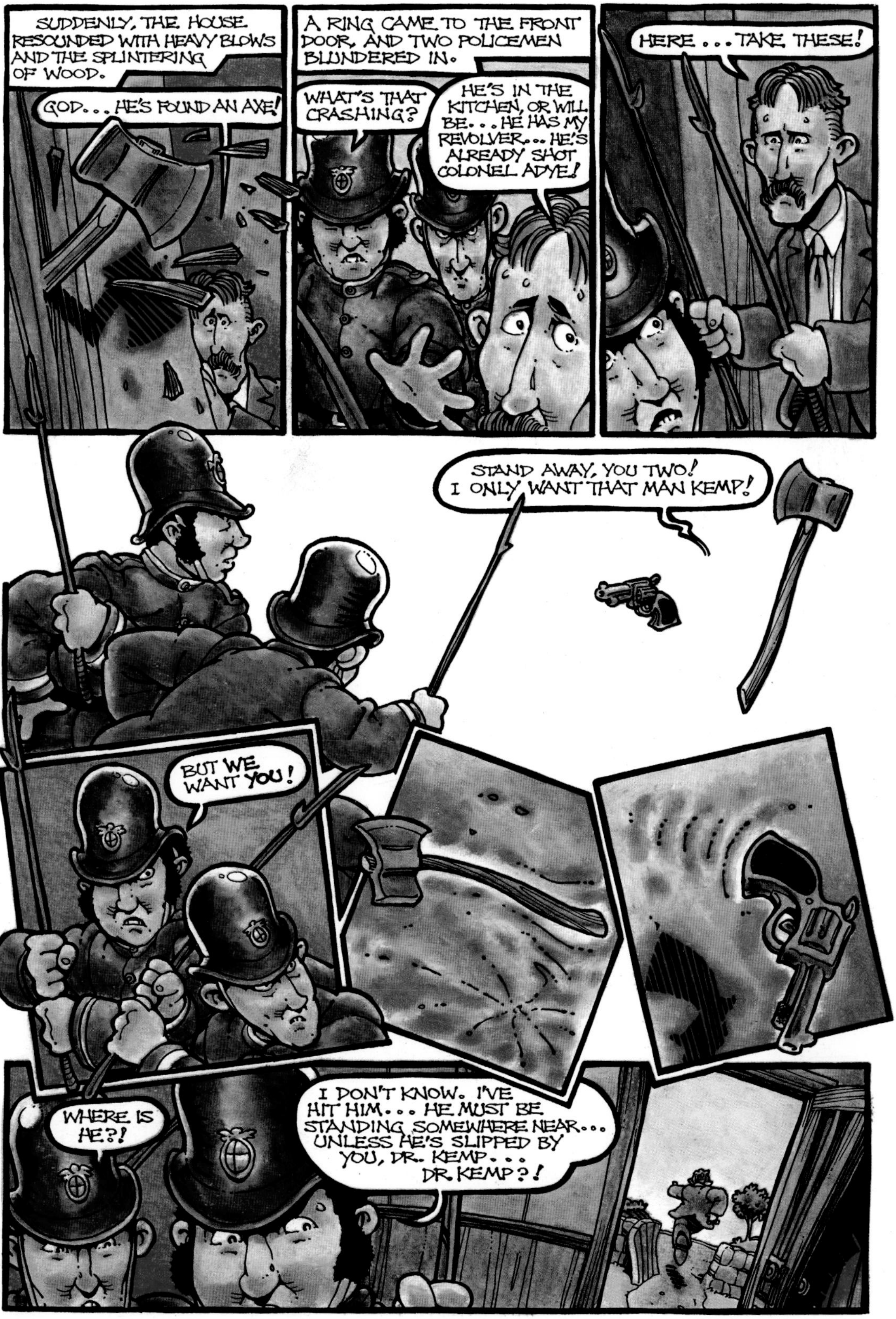
SUDDENLY, THE HOUSE RESOUNDED WITH HEAVY BLOWS AND THE SPLINTERING OF WOOD.
GOD... HE'S FOUND AN AXE!
A RING CAME TO THE FRONT DOOR, AND TWO POLICEMEN BLUNDERED IN.
WHAT'S THAT CRASHING?
HE'S IN THE KITCHEN, OR WILL BE... HE HAS MY REVOLVER... HE'S ALREADY SHOT COLONEL ADYE!
HERE... TAKE THESE!
STAND AWAY, YOU TWO! I ONLY WANT THAT MAN KEMP!
BUT WE WANT YOU!
WHERE IS HE?!
I DON'T KNOW. I'VE HIT HIM... HE MUST BE STANDING SOMEWHERE NEAR... UNLESS HE'S SLIPPED BY YOU, DR. KEMP...
DR. KEMP?!

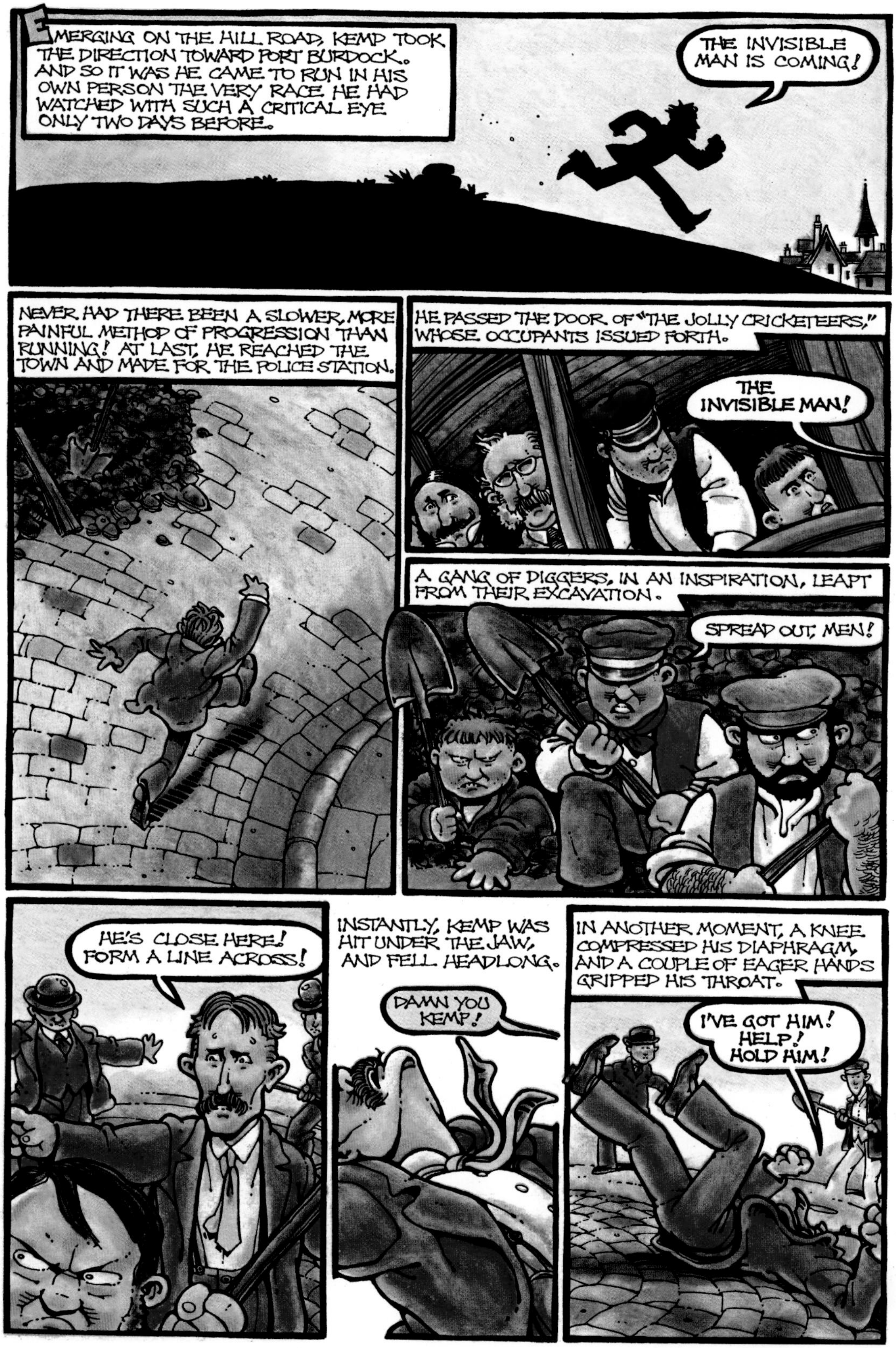
EMERGING ON THE HILL ROAD, KEMP TOOK THE DIRECTION TOWARD PORT BURDOCK. AND SO IT WAS HE CAME TO RUN IN HIS OWN PERSON THE VERY RACE HE HAD WATCHED WITH SUCH A CRITICAL EYE ONLY TWO DAYS BEFORE.
THE INVISIBLE MAN IS COMING!
NEVER HAD THERE BEEN A SLOWER, MORE PAINFUL METHOD OF PROGRESSION THAN RUNNING! AT LAST, HE REACHED THE TOWN AND MADE FOR THE POLICE STATION.
HE PASSED THE DOOR OF "THE JOLLY CRICKETEERS," WHOSE OCCUPANTS ISSUED FORTH.
THE INVISIBLE MAN!
A GANG OF DIGGERS, IN AN INSPIRATION, LEAPT FROM THEIR EXCAVATION.
SPREAD OUT, MEN!
HE'S CLOSE HERE! FORM A LINE ACROSS!
INSTANTLY, KEMP WAS HIT UNDER THE JAW, AND FELL HEADLONG.
DAMN YOU KEMP!
IN ANOTHER MOMENT, A KNEE COMPRESSED HIS DIAPHRAGM, AND A COUPLE OF EAGER HANDS GRIPPED HIS THROAT.
I'VE GOT HIM! HELP! HOLD HIM!

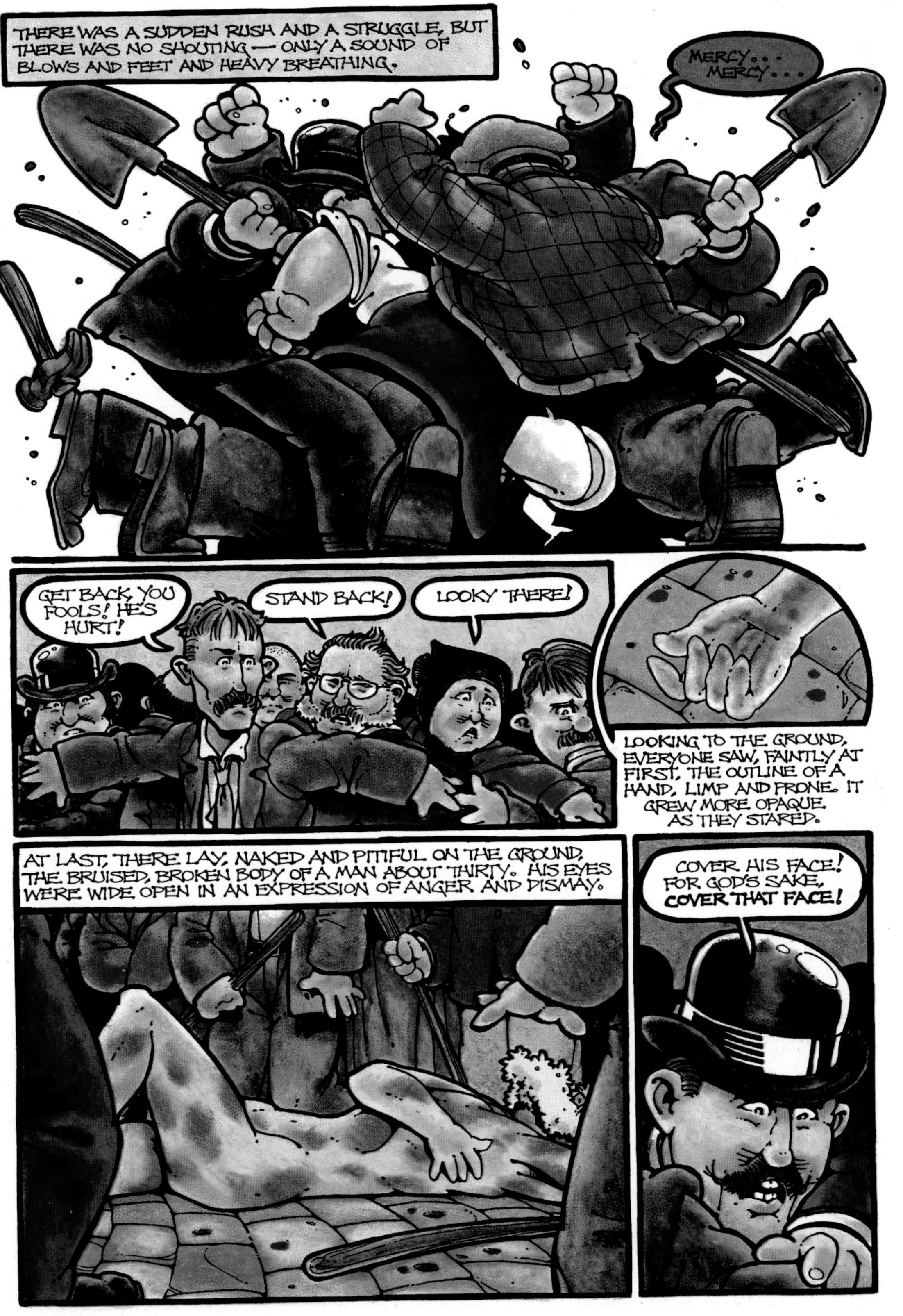
THERE WAS A SUDDEN RUSH AND A STRUGGLE, BUT THERE WAS NO SHOUTING — ONLY A SOUND OF BLOWS AND FEET AND HEAVY BREATHING.
MERCY... MERCY...
GET BACK, YOU FOOLS! HE'S HURT!
STAND BACK!
LOOKY THERE!
LOOKING TO THE GROUND, EVERYONE SAW, FAINTLY AT FIRST, THE OUTLINE OF A HAND, LIMP AND PRONE. IT GREW MORE OPAQUE AS THEY STARED.
AT LAST, THERE LAY, NAKED AND PITIFUL ON THE GROUND, THE BRUISED, BROKEN BODY OF A MAN ABOUT THIRTY. HIS EYES WERE WIDE OPEN IN AN EXPRESSION OF ANGER AND DISMAY.
COVER HIS FACE! FOR GOD'S SAKE, COVER THAT FACE!

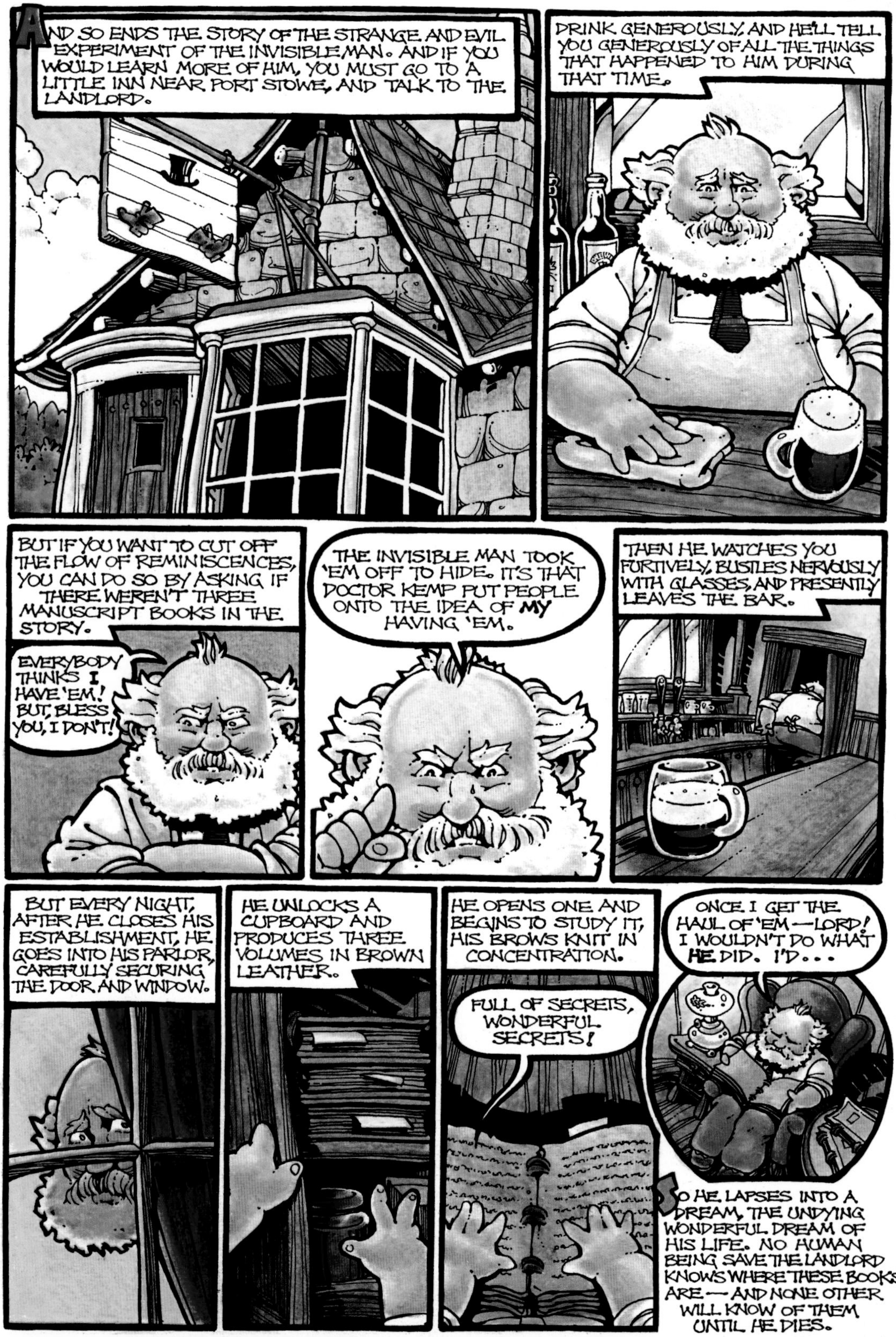
AND SO ENDS THE STORY OF THE STRANGE AND EVIL EXPERIMENT OF THE INVISIBLE MAN. AND IF YOU WOULD LEARN MORE OF HIM, YOU MUST GO TO A LITTLE INN NEAR PORT STOWE, AND TALK TO THE LANDLORD.
DRINK GENEROUSLY, AND HE'LL TELL YOU GENEROUSLY OF ALL THE THINGS THAT HAPPENED TO HIM DURING THAT TIME.
BUT IF YOU WANT TO CUT OFF THE FLOW OF REMINISCENCES, YOU CAN DO SO BY ASKING IF THERE WEREN'T THREE MANUSCRIPT BOOKS IN THE STORY.
EVERYBODY THINKS I HAVE 'EM! BUT, BLESS YOU, I DON'T!
THE INVISIBLE MAN TOOK 'EM OFF TO HIDE. IT'S THAT DOCTOR KEMP PUT PEOPLE ONTO THE IDEA OF MY HAVING 'EM.
THEN HE WATCHES YOU FURTIVELY, BUSTLES NERVOUSLY WITH GLASSES, AND PRESENTLY LEAVES THE BAR.
BUT EVERY NIGHT, AFTER HE CLOSES HIS ESTABLISHMENT, HE GOES INTO HIS PARLOR, CAREFULLY SECURING THE DOOR AND WINDOW.
HE UNLOCKS A CUPBOARD AND PRODUCES THREE VOLUMES IN BROWN LEATHER.
HE OPENS ONE AND BEGINS TO STUDY IT, HIS BROWS KNIT IN CONCENTRATION.
FULL OF SECRETS, WONDERFUL SECRETS!
ONCE I GET THE HAUL OF 'EM — LORD! I WOULDN'T DO WHAT HE DID. I'D...
SO HE LAPSES INTO A DREAM, THE UNDYING WONDERFUL DREAM OF HIS LIFE. NO HUMAN BEING SAVE THE LANDLORD KNOWS WHERE THESE BOOKS ARE — AND NONE OTHER WILL KNOW OF THEM UNTIL HE DIES.

NOW THAT YOU HAVE READ THE CLASSICS Illustrated EDITION, DON'T MISS THE ADDED ENJOYMENT OF READING THE ORIGINAL, OBTAINABLE AT YOUR SCHOOL OR PUBLIC LIBRARY.

WATCH OUT FOR PAPERCUTZ™

Welcome to the second Papercutz edition of CLASSICS ILLUSTRATED. I'm Jim Salicrup, Papercutz Editor-in-Chief, and proud to be associated with such a legendary comicbook series. If you're unfamiliar with Papercutz, let me quickly say that we're the graphic novel publishers of such titles as NANCY DREW, THE HARDY BOYS, TALES FROM THE CRYPT, and now, CLASSICS ILLUSTRATED and CLASSICS ILLUSTRATED DELUXE. In the backpages of our titles, we usually run a section, aptly named "the Papercutz Backpages," which is devoted to letting you know all that's happening at Papercutz. You can also check us out at www.papercutz.com for even more information and previews of upcoming Papercutz graphic novels. But this time around, the big news is CLASSICS ILLUSTRATED!

We'll fill you in on why that's such an awesome big deal in the following pages, but right now I need a moment to take it all in. You see, even though I've been in the world of comics for thirty-five years, I'm still very much the same comicbook fan I was when I was a kid! And if my partner, Papercutz Publisher, Terry Nantier, were to magically go back in time, and tell 13 year-old Jim Salicrup that he was going to one day be the editor of NANCY DREW, THE HARDY BOYS, TALES FROM THE CRYPT, and CLASSICS ILLUSTRATED, he'd think Terry was out of his mind!

Let's get real. Back then I'd see CLASSICS ILLUSTRATED comics in their own display rack, apart from all the other comicbooks, at my favorite soda shoppe in the Bronx. Each issue featured a comics adaptation of a classic novel-that's why they called it CLASSICS ILLUSTRATED. But unlike other comicbooks, these were bigger, containing 48 pages per book; cost a quarter, more than twice as much as a regular 12 cent comic; and stayed on sale forever, as opposed to the other comics which were gone in a month. Clearly, these comics were something special.

Bah, I can take a gazillion moments, but this is still way too humungous an event for my puny brain to fully absorb, so I'm going to give up trying and accept that we here at Papercutz must be doing something right to be entrusted with Comicdom's crown jewels! So no more looking back--time to focus on the future. That means doing everything we can to make sure these titles live up to their proud heritage, while gaining a whole new generation of fans.

As usual, you can contact me at salicrup@papercutz.com or Jim Salicrup, PAPERCUTZ, 40 Exchange Place, Ste. 1308, New York, NY 10005 and let us know how we're doing. After all, we want you to be as excited about Papercutz as we are!

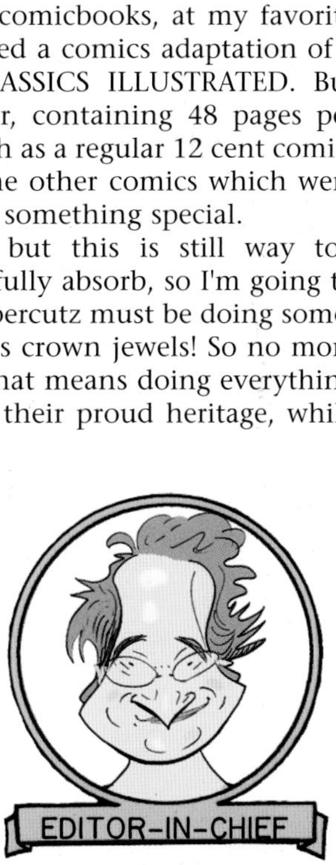
EDITOR-IN-CHIEF

Thanks, Jim

Caricature drawn by Steve Brodner at the MoCCA Art Fest.

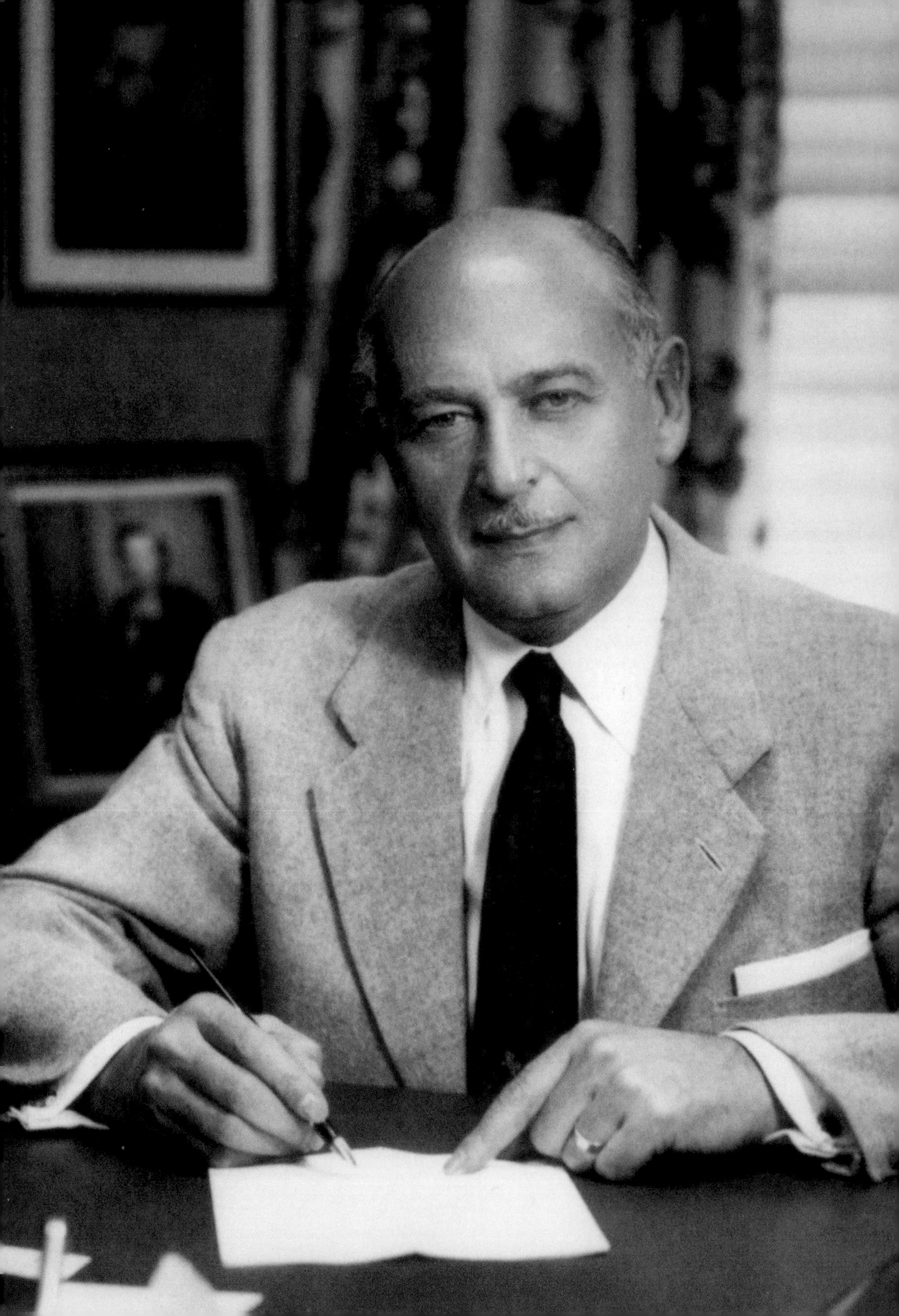

A Short History of CLASSICS ILLUSTRATED...

William B. Jones Jr. is the author of Classics Illustrated: A Cultural History, which offers a comprehensive overview of the original comicbook series and the writers, artists, editors, and publishers behind-the-scenes. With Mr. Jones Jr.'s kind permission, here's a very short overview of the history of CLASSICS ILLUSTRATED from his 2005 essay on Albert Kanter.

CLASSICS ILLUSTRATED was the brainchild of Albert Lewis Kanter, a visionary publisher, who deserves to be ranked among the great teachers of the 20th century. From 1941 to 1971, he introduced young readers to the realms of literature, history, folklore, mythology, and science in such comicbook juvenile series as CLASSICS ILLUSTRATED, CLASSICS ILLUSTRATED JUNIOR, CLASSICS ILLUSTRATED SPECIAL SERIES, and THE WORLD AROUND US.

Born in Baronovitch, Russia on April 11, 1897, Albert Kanter immigrated with his family to the United States in 1904. They settled in Nashua, New Hampshire. A constant reader, Kanter continued to educate himself after leaving high school at the age of sixteen. He worked as a traveling salesman for

Photo of Albert Kanter courtesy of Hal Kanter.

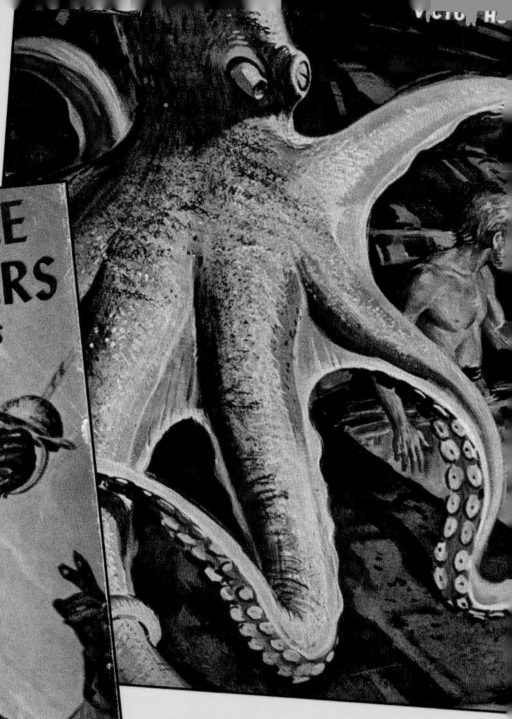

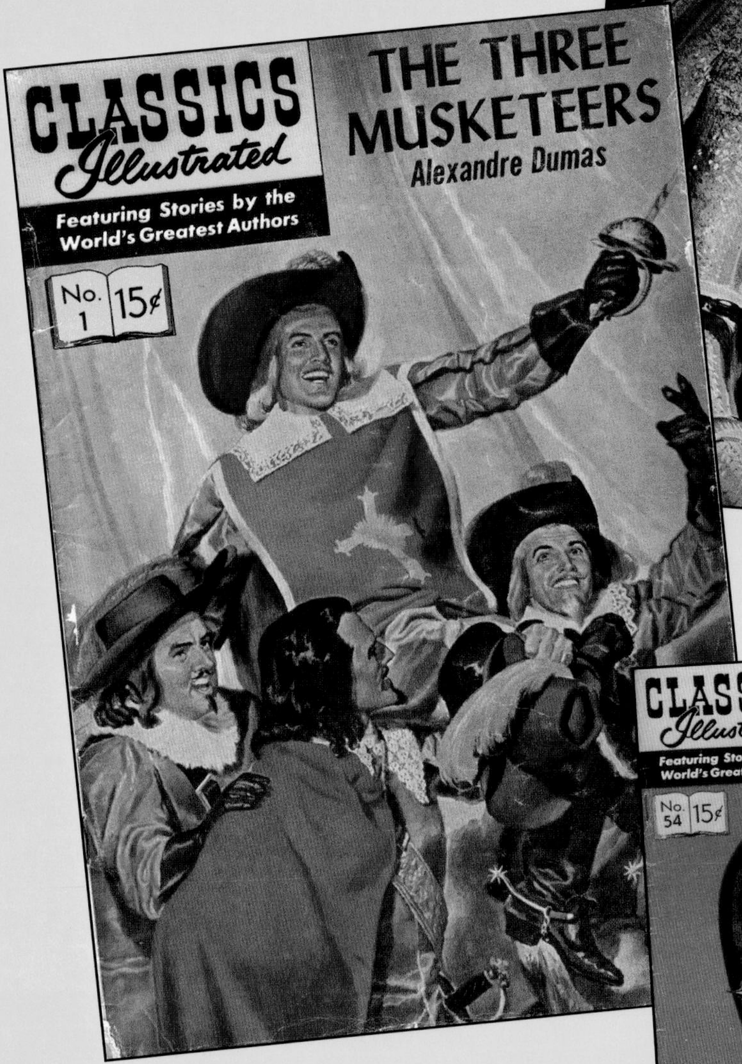
CLASSICS Illustrated
Featuring Stories by the World's Greatest Authors
No. 1 15¢
THE THREE MUSKETEERS
Alexandre Dumas

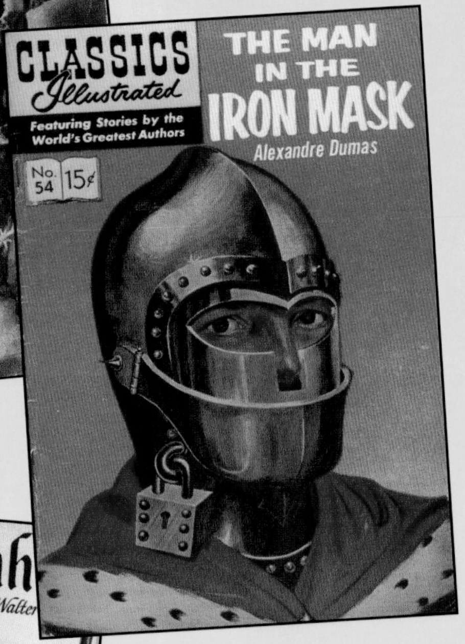
CLASSICS Illustrated
Featuring Stories by the World's Greatest Authors
No. 54 15¢
THE MAN IN THE IRON MASK
Alexandre Dumas

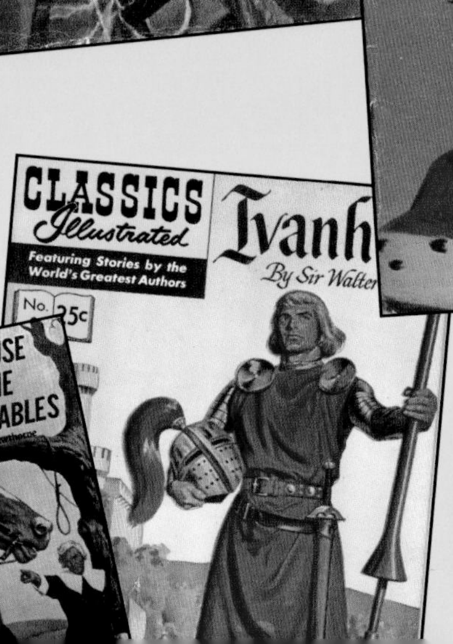
CLASSICS Illustrated
Featuring Stories by the World's Greatest Authors
No. 25c
Ivanh
By Sir Walter

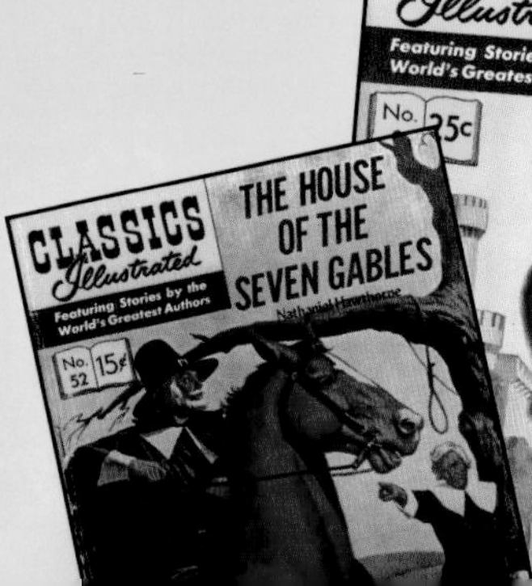
CLASSICS Illustrated
Featuring Stories by the World's Greatest Authors
No. 52 15¢
THE HOUSE OF THE SEVEN GABLES

several years. In 1917, he married Rose Ehrenrich, and the couple lived in Savannah, Georgia, where they had three children, Henry (Hal), William, and Saralea.

They spent several years in Miami, Florida but when the Great Depression ended his real estate venture there, Kanter moved his family to New York. He was employed by the Colonial Press and later the Elliot Publishing Company. During this period, Kanter also designed a popular appointment diary for doctors and dentists and created a toy telegraph and a crystal radio set.

During the late 1930s and early 1940s, millions of youngsters thrilled to the exploits of the new comicbook superheroes. In 1940, Elliot Publishing Company began issuing repackaged pairs of remaindered comics, which sparked a concept in Kanter's mind about a different kind of comicbook. Kanter believed that he could use the same medium to introduce young readers to the world of great literature.

With the backing of two business partners, Kanter launched CLASSIC COMICS in October 1941 with issue No. 1, a comics-style adaptation of *The Three Musketeers*. From the beginning, the series stood apart from other comicbook lines. Each issue was devoted to a different literary work such as *Ivanhoe, Moby Dick*, and *A Tale of Two Cities*, and featured a biography of the author and educational fillers. No outside advertising appeared on the covers or pages. And instead of disappearing after a month on the newsstand, titles were reprinted on a regular basis and listed by number in each issue.

When the new publication outgrew the space it shared with Elliot in 1942, Kanter moved the operation and, under the Gilberton Company corporate name, CLASSIC COMICS entered a period of growing readership and increasing recognition as an educational tool. Kanter worked tirelessly to promote his product and protect its image. In 1947, a "newer, truer" name was given to the monthly series – CLASSICS ILLUSTRATED.

Soon, Kanter's comicbook adaptations of works by Shakespeare, Stevenson, Twain, Verne, and other authors, were being used in schools and endorsed by educators. The series was translated and distributed in numerous foreign countries (including Canada, Great Britain, the Netherlands, Greece, Brazil, Mexico, and Australia) and the genial publisher was hailed abroad as "Papa Klassiker." By the beginning of the 1960s, CLASSICS ILLUSTRATED was the largest

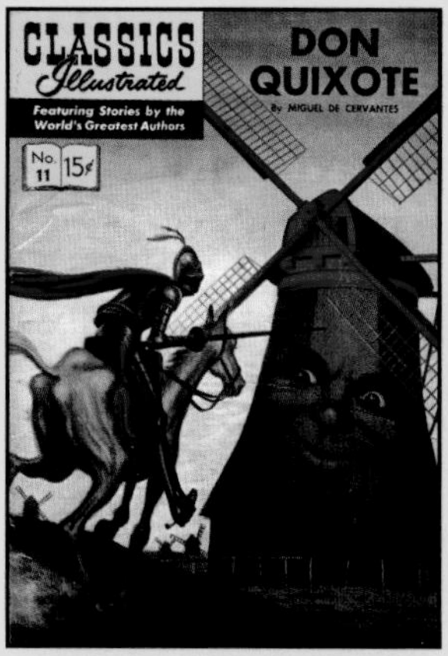
CLASSICS Illustrated
Featuring Stories by the World's Greatest Authors
No. 11 15¢
DON QUIXOTE
By MIGUEL DE CERVANTES

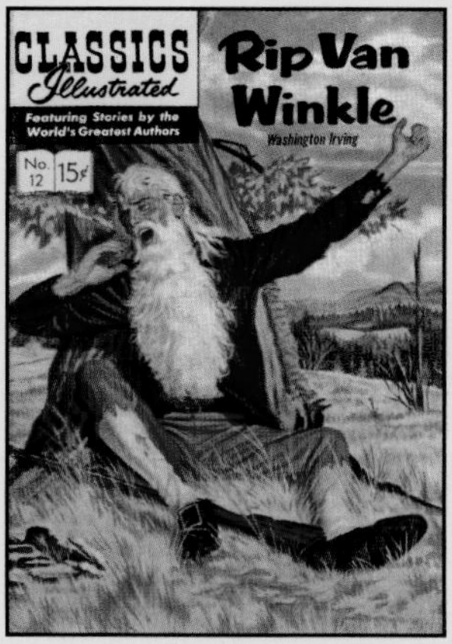
CLASSICS Illustrated
Featuring Stories by the World's Greatest Authors
No. 12 15¢
Rip Van Winkle
Washington Irving

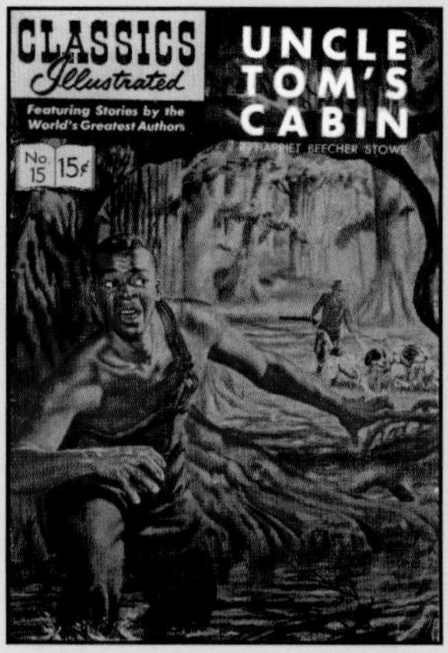
CLASSICS Illustrated
Featuring Stories by the World's Greatest Authors
No. 15 15¢
UNCLE TOM'S CABIN

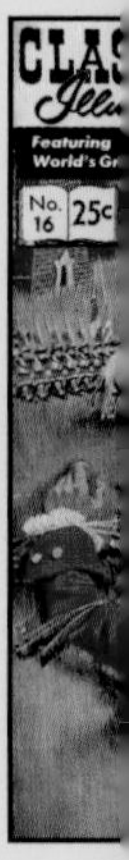
No. 16 25c

juvenile publication in the world. The U.S.-Canadian CLASSICS ILLUSTRATED series would eventually feature 169 titles; among these were *Frankenstein, 20,000 Leagues Under the Sea, Treasure Island, Julius Caesar*, and *Faust*.

In 1953, Kanter sought to reach a younger readership with CLASSICS ILLUSTRATED JUNIOR. The first issue was *Snow White and the Seven Dwarfs*, released October 1953. Eventually, seventy-seven titles would be published. CLASSICS ILLUSTRATED JUNIOR featured fairy tales (*Cinderella*), folk tales (*Paul Bunyan*), myths (*The Golden Fleece*), and children's literature (*The Wizard of Oz*) in comicbook format. The series proved as successful as the parent line. At its peak, in 1960, the average monthly circulation was 262,000.

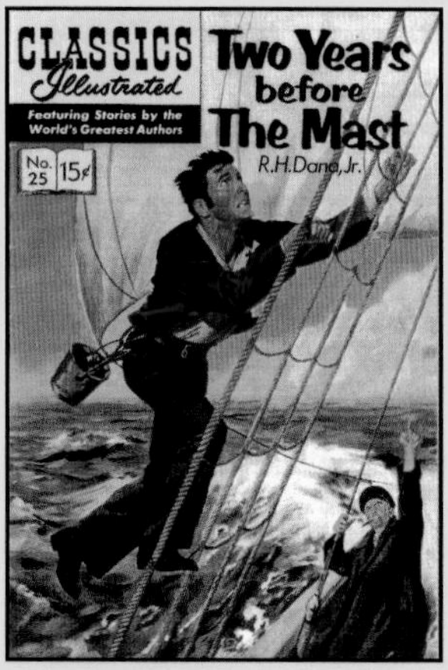
CLASSICS Illustrated
Featuring Stories by the World's Greatest Authors
No. 25 15¢
Two Years before The Mast
R.H.Dana, Jr.

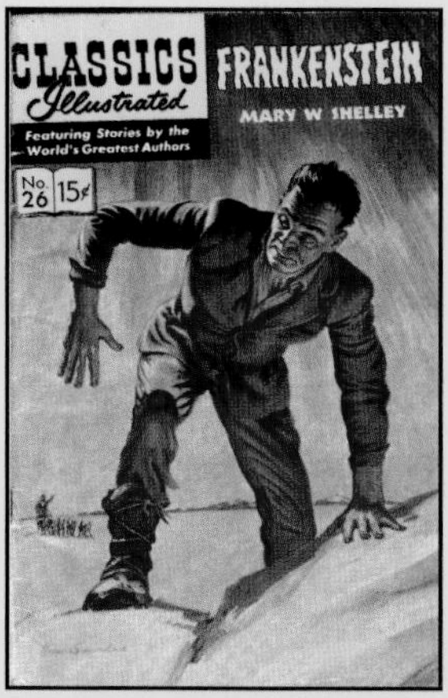
CLASSICS Illustrated
Featuring Stories by the World's Greatest Authors
No. 26 15¢
FRANKENSTEIN
MARY W SHELLEY

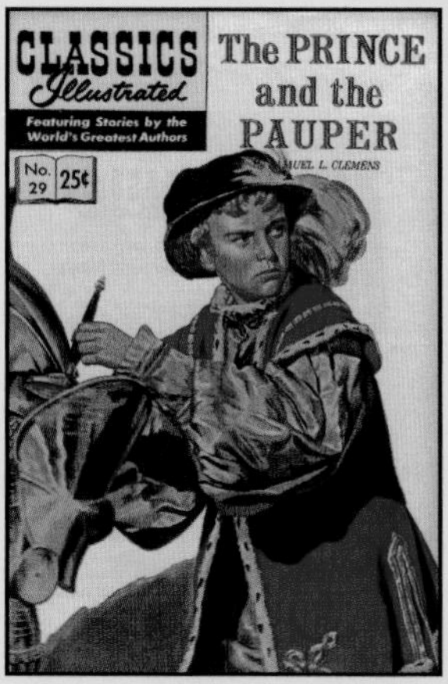
CLASSICS Illustrated
Featuring Stories by the World's Greatest Authors
No. 29 25¢
The PRINCE and the PAUPER

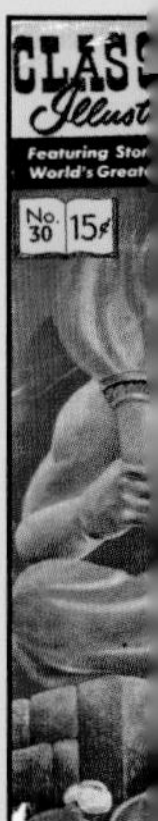
No. 30 15¢

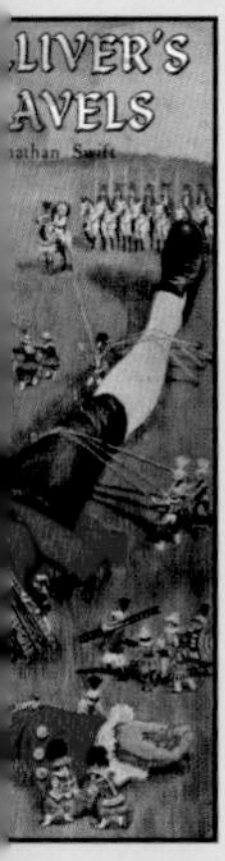
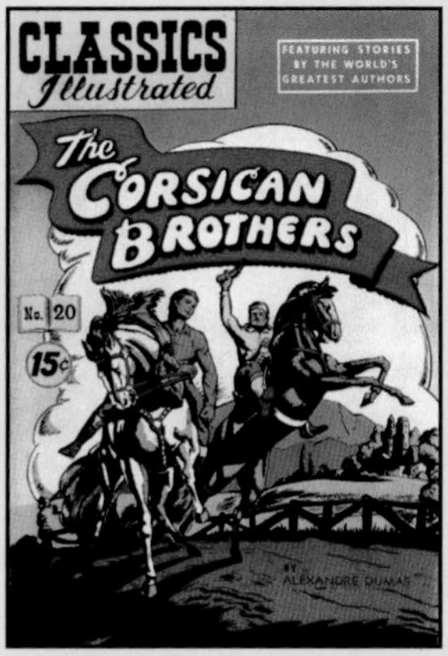
CLASSICS
Illustrated
FEATURING STORIES BY THE WORLD'S GREATEST AUTHORS
The CORSICAN BROTHERS
No. 20
15¢
BY ALEXANDRE DUMAS
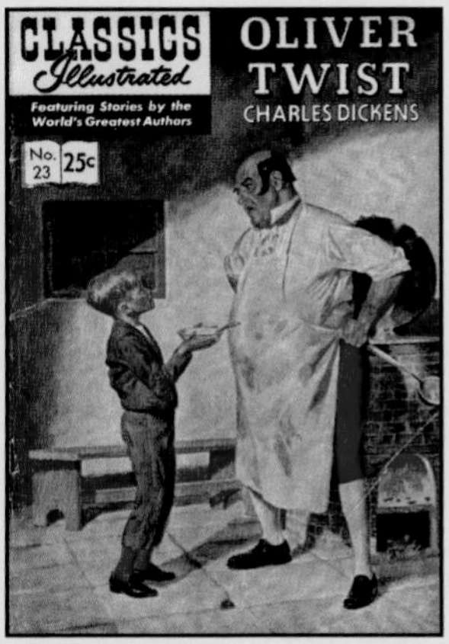
CLASSICS
Illustrated
Featuring Stories by the World's Greatest Authors
OLIVER TWIST
CHARLES DICKENS
No. 23
25¢
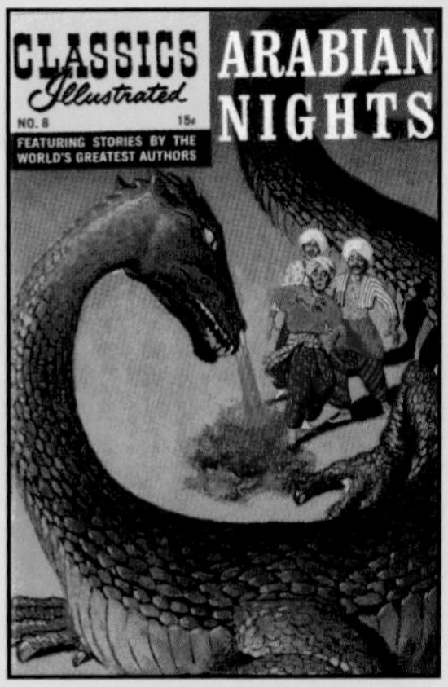
CLASSICS
Illustrated
NO. 8
15¢
FEATURING STORIES BY THE WORLD'S GREATEST AUTHORS
ARABIAN NIGHTS

Kanter continued adding new educational series to the Gilberton Company's line-up. In 1967, he sold the enterprise to Patrick Frawley, who continued publishing CLASSICS ILLUSTRATED and CLASSICS ILLUSTRATED JUNIOR until 1971. After recovering from a stroke in 1970, Kanter and his wife traveled extensively, visiting their grandchildren, other family members, and business associates with whom he shared interests in real estate and his passions for reading, humor, baseball, deep-sea fishing, the theater, and Jewish charities. On March 17, 1973, Albert L. Kanter died, leaving behind a rich legacy for the millions of readers whose imaginations were awakened by CLASSICS ILLUSTRATED and CLASSICS ILLUSTRATED JUNIOR.

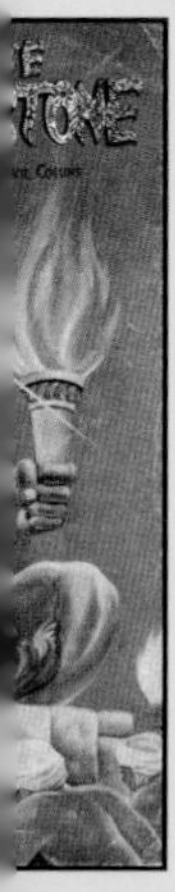
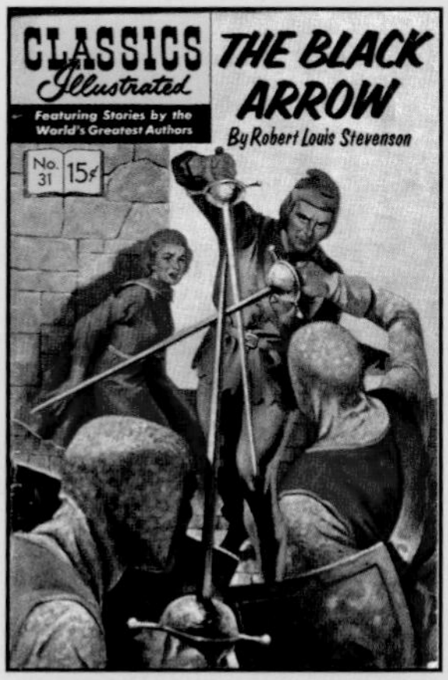
CLASSICS
Illustrated
Featuring Stories by the World's Greatest Authors
THE BLACK ARROW
By Robert Louis Stevenson
No. 31
15¢
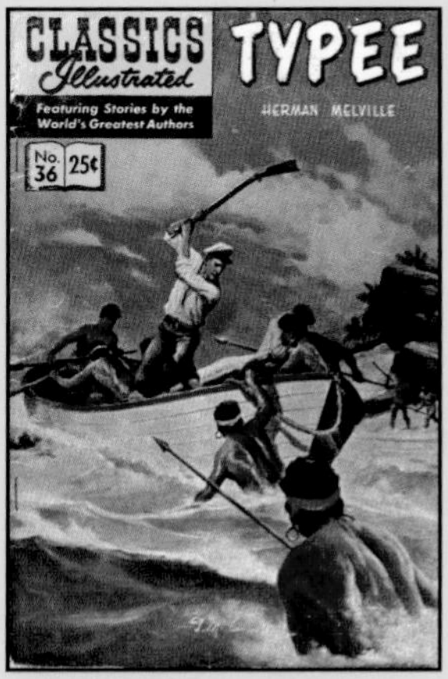
CLASSICS
Illustrated
Featuring Stories by the World's Greatest Authors
TYPEE
HERMAN MELVILLE
No. 36
25¢
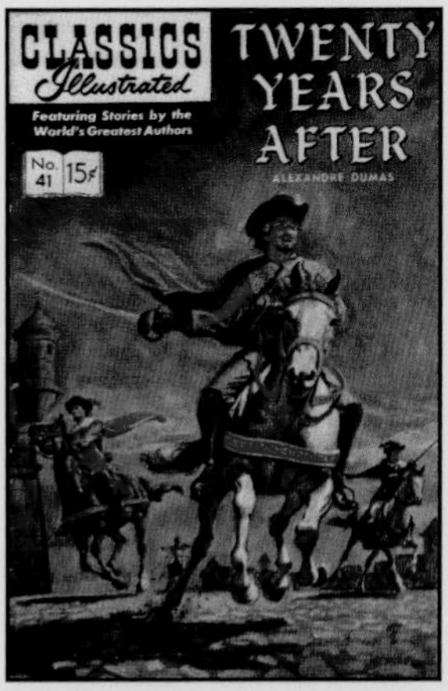
CLASSICS
Illustrated
Featuring Stories by the World's Greatest Authors
TWENTY YEARS AFTER
ALEXANDRE DUMAS
No. 41
15¢

RICK GEARY

Rick Geary was born in 1946 in Kansas City, Missouri and grew up in Wichita, Kansas. He graduated from the University of Kansas in Lawrence, where his first cartoons were published in the University Daily Kansan.

He worked as staff artist for two weekly papers in Wichita before moving to San Diego in 1975.

He began work in comics in 1977 and was for thirteen years a contributor to the Funny Pages of National Lampoon. His comic stories have also been published in Heavy Metal, Dark Horse Comics and the DC Comics/Paradox Press Big Books. His early comic work has been collected in Housebound with Rick Geary from Fantagraphics Books.

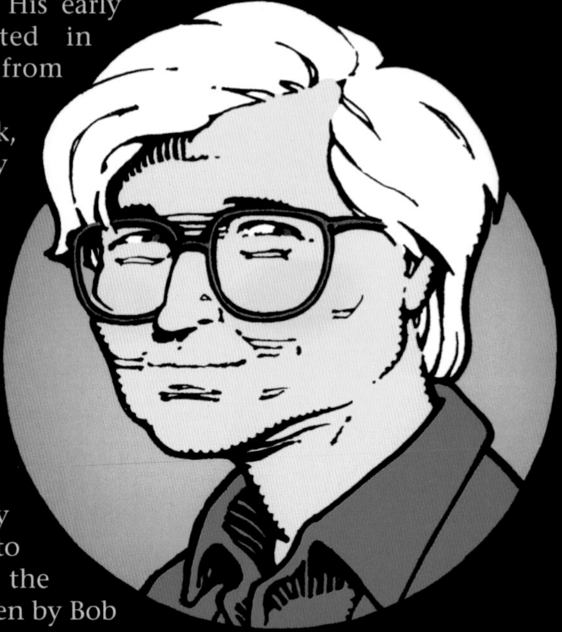

During a four-year stay in New York, his illustrations appeared regularly in The New York Times Book Review. His illustration work has also been seen in MAD, Spy, Rolling Stone, The Los Angeles Times, and American Libraries.

He has written and illustrated three children's books based on The Mask for Dark Horse and two Spider-Man children's books for Marvel. His children's comic Society of Horrors ran in Disney Adventures magazine from 1999 to 2006. He is currently the artist for the new series of Gumby comics, written by Bob Burden.

His graphic novels include three adaptations for CLASSICS ILLUSTRATED and the continuing series A Treasury of Victorian Murder for NBM Publishing, the latest of which is The Saga of the Bloody Benders. In 2007, he wrote and illustrated J. Edgar Hoover: A Graphic Biography for Farrar, Straus and Giroux.

Rick has received the Inkpot Award from the San Diego Comic Convention (1980) and the Book and Magazine Illustration Award from the National Cartoonists Society (1994).

He and his wife Deborah can be found every year in the Artists Alley at San Diego Comic Con International. In 2007, after more than thirty years in San

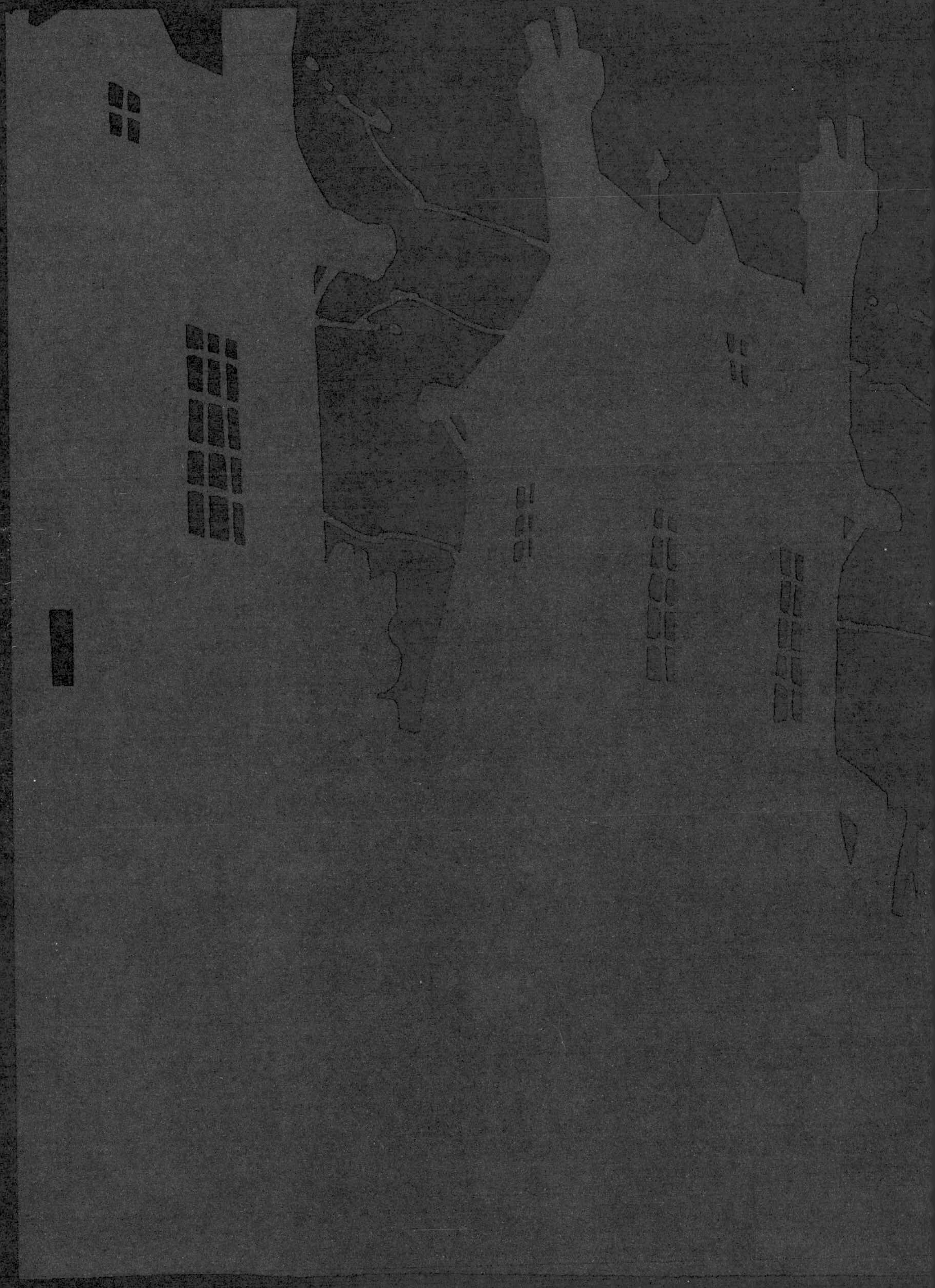